A Note from Stephanie about Meeting Her Pen Pal

I couldn't wait to meet my pen pal, Kyra. We've been writing to each other for so long, it's like we're best friends. I planned to do all kinds of fun things with Kyra, because I figured we liked the exact same things. But when we finally met, boy, was I *wrong!* But first let me tell you about my family.

Right now there are nine people and a dog living in our house—and for all I know, someone new could move in at any time. There's me; my big sister, D.J.; my little sister, Michelle; and my dad, Danny. But that's just the beginning.

Uncle Jesse came first. My dad asked him to come live with us when my mom died, to help take care of me and my sisters.

Back then, Uncle Jesse didn't know much about taking care of three little girls. He was more into rock 'n' roll. So Dad asked his old college buddy, Joey Gladstone, to help out. Joey didn't know anything about kids, either—but it sure was funny watching him learn!

Having Uncle Jesse and Joey around was like having three dads instead of one! But then something even better happened—Uncle Jesse fell in love. He married Becky Donaldson, Dad's co-host on his TV show, *Wake Up, San Francisco*. Aunt Becky's so nice—she's more like a big sister than an aunt.

Next Uncle Jesse and Aunt Becky had twin baby boys. Their names are Nicky and Alex, and they are adorable!

I love being part of a big family. Still, things can get pretty crazy when you live in such a full house!

FULL HOUSE™ STEPHANIE novels

Phone Call from a Flamingo
The Boy-Oh-Boy Next Door
Twin Troubles
Hip Hop Till You Drop
Here Comes the Brand-New Me
The Secret's Out
Daddy's Not-So-Little Girl
P.S. Friends Forever

Available from MINSTREL Books

FULL HOUSE™
Stephanie

P.S. Friends Forever

Devra Newberger Speregen

A Parachute Press Book

A MINSTREL® BOOK

PUBLISHED BY POCKET BOOKS

New York   London   Toronto   Sydney   Tokyo   Singapore

A MINSTREL PAPERBACK *Original*

 A Minstrel Book published by
POCKET BOOKS, a division of Simon & Schuster Inc.
1230 Avenue of the Americas, New York, NY 10020

A Parachute Press Book
Copyright © 1995 by Warner Bros., Inc.

ISBN: 0-671-89861-2

First Minstrel Books printing February 1995

10 9 8 7 6 5 4 3 2 1

Cover photo by Schultz Photography

Printed in the U.S.A.

P.S. Friends Forever

CHAPTER
1

◆ ◄ ◂ ◆

"Don't just sit there!" Stephanie Tanner cried out. She moved uneasily toward her bed, trying to balance an enormous pile of clothing in her arms. Over the top of the pile she could see the unhappy faces of her two best friends, Allie Taylor and Darcy Powell.

"C'mon, guys, give me a hand!"

Allie and Darcy reluctantly got up from Stephanie's bed. Stephanie split the pile in half, giving each of her friends an armful of clothing.

"Stephanie, do you really have to do this *now*?" Darcy asked, blowing a long, dark curl

1

off her face. "I mean, we came over today to have fun. Not to clean out your closet."

Stephanie put her hands on her hips. "I'm not cleaning it out," she corrected her. "I'm just reorganizing it to make room for Kyra. It won't take much longer," she added, scooping up a bunch of sneakers. "So quit whining and put those clothes on Michelle's bed."

Darcy sighed and threw her pile onto Stephanie's younger sister's bed.

"Not like that!" Stephanie shrieked. "You'll wrinkle them!"

"Steph," Allie said calmly, "don't you think you're going a bit overboard?"

But Stephanie didn't seem to hear. She just brushed the stray blond hairs that had escaped from her scrunchie away from her eyes and picked up a brown shoe. "Do you think this needs a shining?" she asked. "I can't see my reflection." She gazed at all the shoes on the closet floor. "Do you think they all need to be shined?"

Allie's pretty green eyes widened in exasperation. "I think she's lost it," she whispered loudly to Darcy.

Darcy nodded. "Completely," she added.

"Well, I can't help it," Stephanie said. "I just want to make sure everything is perfect for Kyra's visit."

Allie tossed her clothing pile onto Michelle's bed, then fell on top of both piles. "Kyra, Kyra, Kyra . . . that's all we've heard you talk about for three weeks now," she moaned. "Kyra hasn't even gotten here yet, and already I've had enough of her."

"Yeah, really, Stephanie," Darcy added. "What's the big deal? She's not going to, like, inspect your closet or anything, is she?"

"No, of course not," Stephanie said. "My father already beat her to it, anyway. I'm just trying to make room for her. She's probably bringing lots of clothes—she's staying for ten days, you know."

"We know! We know!" Darcy and Allie replied in unison.

"Ten days and sixteen hours," Darcy added as if she'd heard this a hundred times already. "And you're going to take her dancing, and to school, and to the Burger Buddy, and—"

"—to the mall," Allie chimed in, "and out for

Chinese, and to your uncle Jesse's next jam session, and—"

"Okay! Okay!" Stephanie groaned. "I get your point." She pulled some more of her clothes off their hangers and sighed. "Yuck. Would you look at these clothes? They're all so . . . *immature.* What's Kyra going to think when she sees how babyish my clothes are?"

Allie put her hands on her hips. "Your clothes are fine, Stephanie," she said. "And, since most of them happen to be mine, I'll try not to take offense at what you said."

Stephanie plopped down on her bed. "I'm sorry, Allie. I didn't mean to insult your clothes or anything. You know I love swapping clothes with you. It's just that I'm so worried about making a good impression on Kyra, that's all. I really want her to like me."

"Kyra *does* like you," Allie said, twisting a piece of her long, light brown hair around her finger. "You guys have been pen pals for almost three years now. If she didn't like you, she would have stopped writing to you a long time ago."

"And she wouldn't be coming to see you, either," Darcy pointed out.

4

Stephanie considered this. "Yeah, I guess."

"She's right, Steph," Allie went on. "You two are so close already. When Kyra steps off that plane, it will be like instant new best friends. You'll see."

"Just don't forget about your *old* best friends," Darcy said with a laugh.

Stephanie smiled and playfully tossed a sneaker at Darcy. "No way," she said. "Oh, wait! I almost forgot. Did I tell you that Kyra said she was bringing me a surprise from Atlanta?"

Allie and Darcy exchanged glances, then burst out laughing.

"Only six times!" Darcy cried.

"Well, fine," Stephanie said. "Keep making jokes, but I'm sure you guys will be totally envious when you see what she gives me. Kyra is just *so* cool. I'll bet it's a new dance tape, or a scary science fiction book. Kyra reads "Star Trek" books, and now I love them, too. It's so weird that Kyra and I have the exact same taste. It's like we were really twins who were separated at birth. Hmmm . . . I'll have to ask my dad about that."

"Ask Dad about what?" Danny Tanner said, coming into the bedroom. He stopped short in front of Stephanie's closet and gasped, clutching his heart. "Steph! Wh-wh-what's going on in here? Your room! Your closet! It's a *mess!*"

"I know, Dad. I told you. I'm reorganizing my closet to make room for Kyra."

Danny gazed unhappily at the piles of clothing all over the room. "Reorganizing?" he repeated. "It looks more like you're having a rummage sale in here."

Stephanie rolled her eyes. "Don't worry, Dad," she assured him. "I'll have it all back to normal by dinnertime." She pushed him lightly, ushering him out of the room.

Danny shook his head. "Okay, okay. I'm going, I'm going," he said. "I have to leave in a few minutes anyway, to make the Thursday night double coupon sale at Cleansers 'R Us. But, sweetie, just do me one favor."

"What, Dad?" Stephanie asked.

"When you put your shoes back on the shoe trees, arrange them by color."

"Dad!"

"I know! I'm going!"

As Danny closed the door behind him, Stephanie put her head in her hands and sighed loudly. "Kyra is going to think my family is nuts!" she wailed.

Allie put her arm around her friend. "No, not nuts," she told her. "A little kooky, maybe, but definitely not nuts."

Stephanie glanced helplessly at her friends, then burst out laughing.

"Hey, is Kyra coming with us to Skate for School night next Friday?" Allie asked.

"Oh, definitely!" Stephanie replied. "Luckily, her school is on a break, and she doesn't have a lot of homework to do. So we can hang out and do everything together. We both love Rollerblading. It's going to be a blast."

"Are you asking anyone to go with you?" Allie asked.

"I told you," Stephanie said, "Kyra is coming with us."

"No," Allie told her, "I mean, are you asking a *guy*?"

Stephanie's eyes widened. "You mean we're supposed to bring *dates*?"

"Well, not exactly," Darcy explained. "But a lot of the seventh-grade girls are making it a big deal and asking guys."

Stephanie made a face. "Well, I'm bringing Kyra!" she exclaimed. "And anyway, what guy would I ask?"

Allie smiled. "A certain tall, hunky soccer player, maybe?" she teased.

"Yeah, like Brandon Fallow might ever go out with me," Stephanie said.

"You never know," Darcy said. "Maybe you should ask him."

"I hope I'm not the only one going without a guy," Stephanie said. "Are you guys asking anyone?"

"Don't look at me!" Allie exclaimed. "I couldn't get up the nerve to ask anyone."

"Me, either," Darcy added. "It looks like you'll be my date!" she said to Allie with a laugh.

"Well, then, the four of us can double-date!" Stephanie exclaimed. "It'll be great. Wait a sec, that reminds me. Did I tell you Kyra said in her letter she has a crush on a guy in her class?"

"Actually, Stephanie, *that* you haven't told us!" Darcy proclaimed.

Stephanie grinned and took Kyra's latest letter out of her desk drawer. It was hidden under a pile of old notebooks—just in case Michelle went snooping around. Stephanie had opened and read it so many times since it came three weeks before, the pages were practically falling apart. She'd already read parts of the letter a few times to Allie and Darcy.

"Listen," she said. Clearing her throat, she read aloud. " 'Dear Stephanie, Hey! What's up? How are—' "

"Steph! We've heard this part already! Get to the part about the crush," Darcy said.

Stephanie scanned the pages until she found what she was looking for. "Okay, here it is. 'So, anyway, Steph, did I tell you about this guy who sits next to me in homeroom? He's drop-dead gorgeous. I like him even better than Billy Strummer.' " Stephanie looked up from the letter. "Billy Strummer is this guy Kyra had a crush on last summer." She went back to the letter. " 'So what do you think, Betty? Should I talk to him?' "

Allie scrunched up her nose. "Betty?" she asked.

Stephanie laughed. "Yeah, Kyra calls me Betty and I call her Wilma. We're both big Flintstones fans."

"Anyway," Stephanie went on, "listen to this part. Kyra says she wants me to come visit her in Atlanta for two weeks this summer."

"Wow! Do you think your dad will let you go?" Darcy asked.

"I hope so. I haven't asked him yet," Stephanie said with a frown. She carefully folded the letter and put it back in its hiding place. Then she dropped to her knees and went back to reorganizing her closet.

"Just remind him about your excellent report card last quarter," Allie told her as she handed Stephanie a shoe.

"Yeah, and promise him you'll reorganize *his* closet or something," Darcy added.

Stephanie and Allie looked around the room at the mess of clothes on the floor, then back at Darcy.

"Okay, maybe not," Darcy said with a laugh.

CHAPTER
2

◆ ◀ ✦ ◆

After school on Friday, Stephanie sat in her room, trying to get up the nerve to ask her father about going to Atlanta. Finally, she got an idea. She found the *Wake Up, San Francisco* sweatshirt he'd given her last Christmas and put it on. Then she brushed her hair in the style she knew he liked and went downstairs to find him.

In the living room Stephanie's entire family was gathered around the television, laughing hysterically.

"Hey, what's going on down here?" Stephanie asked loudly.

"Shhhh!" Her older sister, D.J., waved at her to be quiet.

"We're watching this *Sesame Street* special with Nicky and Alex," Stephanie's aunt Becky whispered in between giggles. "It's hilarious!" Stephanie's aunt Becky and uncle Jesse and their twin toddler boys lived in the attic apartment upstairs.

"Ha!" Jesse shouted. "Check out Cookie Monster's Elvis impersonation. It's almost as good as mine."

"It's better," Danny pointed out.

"Much better," Michelle added.

"Uh, excuse me, but just one thing," Stephanie told them all.

"What is it, Steph?" Joey asked impatiently. Joey Gladstone was her dad's best friend from college. He moved in with the Tanners after Stephanie's mother died.

"Make it quick," Joey added. "Kermit's big number is coming up."

"What I wanted to say," Stephanie told them, "is that Nicky and Alex aren't even here."

Everyone stopped laughing at once and looked around the room for the three-year-olds.

"Becky, I thought you were watching them!" Jesse said, jumping up to check under the sofa for his sons.

"Uh-uh, Jess, it was your turn," Becky replied, racing to check the closet under the stairs.

Everyone began frantically searching for the missing twins.

Danny ran into the kitchen, then poked his head back into the living room. He had a huge grin on his face. "Hey, guys, come here. You have to see this," he whispered loudly.

Everyone lined up at the door to the kitchen and peered in.

"Oh, aren't they sweet!" Becky exclaimed quietly. "The boys are setting the dinner table for us." She laughed as her sons placed toy cups and plates around the huge kitchen table.

Joey laughed. "Now, isn't that something," he said. "The toddlers are getting dinner ready while the grown-ups watch *Sesame Street*. Boy, do I feel like a dork!"

Everyone laughed.

"Joey!" Michelle called out. "Kermit's on."

"Out of my way!" Joey pushed past everyone to get to the television.

13

Stephanie followed her father into the kitchen. He was taking dinner out of the oven.

"Smells great, Dad," she said excitedly.

"Thanks, hon," he said. "How's the closet coming along?"

"Fine, just fine," she replied. "I have the most organized shoes on the block."

Danny smiled. "I'm so proud. Oh, and you're wearing the sweatshirt I gave you last Christmas. It looks darling on you."

Stephanie mustered up a smile. "Uh, Dad?" she asked.

"What is it, Steph?"

Stephanie bit her bottom lip. "Can I . . . can I . . . can I help you with dinner?" she asked nervously.

"That's all right, Steph. I have it under control."

"Oh, okay. Uh, Dad?" Stephanie asked again.

Danny sighed. "What, Stephanie?"

She hesitated. "Maybe you need a load of laundry done or something?"

Danny put down his oven mitt. "All right, Stephanie," he said, folding his arms across his chest. "What's going on? What do you want?"

"What makes you think I want something?" Stephanie asked innocently.

"I can spot the buttering-up-Dad routine from a mile away," Danny said. "D.J. had it down to a science before I caught on."

"Darn," Stephanie muttered under her breath.

"So what is it?" Danny asked impatiently. "A later curfew? Your own room? What?"

"Okay," Stephanie said finally. "Here it is. I'll just come right out and ask. No beating around the bush. Just one, two, three, and I'll say it. There's no time like the—"

"Stephanie!"

"Okay, okay," she said. She closed her eyes, held her breath, crossed her fingers, and blurted it out. "Can I go to Atlanta for two weeks this summer?"

Danny took a large bowl of salad from the fridge and carried it to the table.

"Listen, hon," he said quietly. "I'd love to send you to Atlanta—"

Stephanie's eyes shot open. She gasped and smiled an enormous smile. "Really? Oh, thank you!" she cried, jumping up and down happily. "Thank you! You're the best dad in the whole world. I was just telling Darcy and Allie yesterday what a great dad you were and that how of course you would let me go visit Kyra and—"

"Whoa! Wait a minute, Stephanie. I didn't finish. I was going to say I would love to send you to Atlanta, but—"

"There's a but?" Stephanie asked suddenly. "That's not good. Buts are never good."

"But," her father continued, "I'm planning a big Tanner family vacation this summer and it's going to cost a lot of money. I'm afraid you can take only one summer vacation this year, Steph."

Stephanie slumped her shoulders and hung her head.

"I'm sorry, honey," her father said gently. "But if I let you go to Georgia, then I have to let D.J. go to Florida. And Michelle to the North Pole."

Stephanie's eyes narrowed. "The North Pole?" she asked.

Danny smiled. "Michelle said she wants to visit Santa during the summer so he doesn't get too lonely."

Stephanie rolled her eyes. "But, Dad—"

"Sorry, Steph. I can't afford to send everybody on separate vacations."

Stephanie sighed. "All right, Dad. I understand," she replied unhappily. She left the kitchen and walked slowly through the living room, where Joey and Michelle were still watching television.

"What's the matter, Stephanie?" Michelle asked.

"Dad won't let me go to Atlanta," she replied grumpily. "I wanted to visit Kyra."

"Where's Atlanta?" Michelle asked.

"Might as well be in China," Stephanie answered.

"Where's Atlanta?" Michelle asked again.

"It's in Georgia, Michelle," Joey said.

"Well, I know a way Stephanie can go to Atlanta!" Michelle said to Joey. "But since she's such a meanie, I'm not going to tell her!"

"What are you talking about, Michelle?" Stephanie asked.

Michelle folded her arms across her chest.

Stephanie sighed. "Come on, Michelle. I'm sorry I didn't answer your question. Just tell me what you know."

Michelle thought for a moment, then pointed to the television. "You can *win* a trip to Atlanta!" she announced, sitting back triumphantly.

"What do you mean?" Stephanie asked.

"Joey and I saw a commercial for rice cakes,"

Michelle explained. "Georgia Peach Rice Cakes. And they're having a contest to win a trip to Georgia for a tour of their rice cake factory."

Stephanie narrowed her eyes at Michelle. "You're kidding, right?"

"Nope. Ask Joey if you don't believe me."

Stephanie looked at Joey suspiciously. "Joey, is she joking?"

"No joke, Steph," Joey said. "She's telling the truth. The grand prize is a trip to Georgia for one week and all the rice cakes you can eat."

"How do I enter?" Stephanie asked impatiently.

"They said the entry forms are on the back of the rice cake packages," Joey told her.

Stephanie clasped her hands together excitedly. "This is awesome!" she exclaimed happily. "I'll buy a hundred packages and enter a hundred times! I'll definitely win!" She flopped down on the sofa in between Joey and her sister.

"Guess what, guys?" she said, batting her eyes and doing her best southern accent. "Ahm goin' t'Geawgah!"

In school on Monday, Stephanie waited impatiently for Allie and Darcy to join her at their regular lunch table in the cafeteria. She'd missed them that morning at their usual meeting place. Finally, she spotted Allie's scarlet and gold 49ers sweatshirt in the cafeteria line. Stephanie jumped up from the table and ran over, cutting into the line to talk to Allie.

"Hey!" a sixth-grade boy said angrily. "No cutting in."

"Cool your jets, bub," Stephanie snapped at him. "I'm not in line." She turned back to Allie. "You got 'em?" she asked eagerly.

Allie made a face. "Chill out, Stephanie! Yes, I have them. But can I get my juice first?"

"Oh, yeah, of course," Stephanie said. "How many do you have?"

"Three," Allie answered, putting a container of orange juice on her lunch tray.

"Three?" Stephanie cried out in disappointment. "Just three? How am I supposed to win this contest with only three entry forms? What happened? I thought you were going to get ten!"

"Give me a break, Stephanie. Three packages of rice cakes were all I could afford. Have you tasted those things? They're *awful*."

"They're not so bad," Stephanie mumbled.

"Are you kidding? They taste like Styrofoam."

Darcy cut in front of them. "You must be talking about those Georgia Peach Rice Cakes," she said with a grimace. "Boy, are they yuck-o, or what?"

The sixth-grade boy pointed at Darcy and yelled. "Hey! You cut in! I saw you!"

"Don't worry," Darcy snapped at him, "I'm not buying anything." She turned back to Stephanie. "Anyway, those cakes taste like cardboard."

"Oh, come on, they aren't *that* bad," Stephanie said. "You just have to put some stuff on them to make them taste better. They're really healthy for you," she pointed out.

Darcy and Allie were silent.

"And they're fat-free, too," Stephanie added, making one last effort to win them over.

"Big deal," Darcy stated. "They stink."

"Oh, come on, you guys," Stephanie wailed. "Please keep eating them. Please? The only way to get those entry forms is from the packages. I have to win that trip. I have to!"

Darcy made a gagging noise. "Well, I suppose

I could choke a few more down," she said. "Since it's for a good cause."

Allie smiled. "Yeah, so what if we have to be rushed to the hospital with major stomach pains? As long as you can go to Georgia, Stephanie, it will all be worth it."

"Ha-ha," Stephanie answered. "But, really, thank you, guys. Darcy, how many entry forms do you have?"

"I could get my mom to buy only two packages of them," she said. "But I'll get more this week."

"Okay," Stephanie said, calculating out loud. "Yours and Allie's make five altogether, plus Joey's four, Dad's three, and my five—that makes seventeen. I better get to work on D.J., Aunt Becky, and Uncle Jesse. Michelle doesn't have any money, so I guess I'll have to let that go."

"Wow, that's really nice of you," Darcy muttered sarcastically. She put a carton of apple juice on Allie's tray.

"Hey!" the sixth grader yelled at her. "You're buying something. I saw you take that juice."

Darcy and Stephanie glared at him.

"Uh, well, it's okay. Help yourself," he said meekly, backing away from their stares.

Allie pulled her friends toward the cashier. "Come on, let's sit down."

"You're not buying lunch today, Steph?" Allie asked after they sat down.

Stephanie smiled uneasily and produced a brown paper bag. "Uh, no, I brought lunch today," she said with a groan. "Salami on rice cake sandwich."

"Mmmmm," Darcy said, clutching her throat and grimacing. "Sounds tasty!"

"Well, Dad made me promise I'd eat them," Stephanie said. "I had to talk him into buying the three bags somehow. Anyway, listen, you two. Don't tell Kyra anything about the contest and my trip to Atlanta, okay? I want it to be a surprise."

"Uh, Stephanie," Allie said, "aren't you jumping the gun a bit? I mean, you haven't won the contest yet, you know."

"Yeah, and you might not win," Darcy added.

"Of course I will," Stephanie insisted. "I have to win. I'll bet nobody else is going to enter as many times as me. I *have* to win!"

Darcy shrugged. "Whatever you say."

"Really," Stephanie said. "I just have this feeling, you know? I want to win so bad, I'm thinking only positively. Hey, did I tell you Kyra got a perm?"

Darcy put her head down on the table and groaned loudly.

Allie nodded. "Yes, Steph. You told us."

"Well, I can't wait to see it," Stephanie said. "Maybe I'll get one, too."

"But your hair is so great the way it is," Darcy said, lifting her head. "You have the best hair in the seventh grade. Why would you want to change it?"

"Maybe it's time for a change," Stephanie replied. "And Kyra just got a second hole pierced in her ear, too. Did I tell you?"

Darcy and Allie both nodded without looking up from their lunches.

"Well, that must be totally cool," Stephanie went on. "I always wanted to get another hole done."

Allie took a swig of her juice. "You said two holes looked stupid," she reminded her. "Remember that girl at the mall with the two big hoop earrings in one ear? You said that was gross."

"That *was* gross," Stephanie replied. "But I meant the two earrings the size of basketball hoops, not the two holes. And anyway, Kyra says it's all the rage in Atlanta."

"Big whoop," Darcy muttered.

Stephanie ignored her. "So, anyway, do you think I should get tickets for me and Kyra to see a Warriors game?"

Allie shrugged. "I don't know, Stephanie. Why don't you wait until Kyra gets here and see what she wants to do?"

Stephanie laughed. "Oh, I'm sure Kyra will *love* going to a basketball game."

"I know, I know, Steph, but shouldn't you wait, just to be sure?"

Stephanie sat back in her chair thoughtfully. "Maybe," she said. "Anyway, wait until she sees what I have planned for this Saturday. We're going to tour all of San Francisco! Uncle Jesse is taking us to Fisherman's Wharf for clam chowder."

"It sounds like fun," Darcy agreed. "Does Kyra like chowder?"

Stephanie scoffed. "Of course she does," she answered. "If I like it, Kyra likes it. So what should I wear to the airport on Thursday night?"

Allie stared at her friend in amazement. "You're kidding, right?"

"No, I'm not kidding! I want to wear something really, oh, I don't know, something really *me*. Wait, I know. I'll borrow D.J.'s khaki overalls."

"But that's not really you," Darcy pointed out. "That's really D.J."

Stephanie made a face. "Well, I wear overalls, too, you know. And anyway," she added with a laugh, "I'll bet Kyra will step off the plane and we'll be wearing the same exact thing. I'm telling you, we're so much alike, it's spooky. Did I tell you that Kyra has the same glasses as me, too?"

Allie and Darcy groaned.

CHAPTER
3

◆ ◀ ▪ ◆

"Dad, are you sure we're waiting in the right place?" Stephanie asked. She stood with her nose pressed up against the glass window at the Gate 7 waiting area, which was overlooking the airfield. She hoped to catch sight of Kyra's plane.

"Stephanie, will you relax? You've asked me that a hundred times already. Yes, we're in the right place. Kyra's plane should be here any minute."

"Oooh, I can hardly wait!" Stephanie exclaimed happily. "I can't believe we're actually going to meet face-to-face."

Danny nodded. "You must be pretty excited."

Just then, there was an announcement. "Now arriving at Gate 7, Flight 026 from Atlanta, Georgia."

"That's her!" Stephanie grabbed her father's arm and pulled him all the way to the door to Gate 7. "Hurry!"

Stephanie watched anxiously as each passenger came through the gate. Nervously, she played with her friendship bracelet as she scanned the crowd of passengers.

When the last passenger came through the gate, Stephanie turned to her father in a panic.

"Where is she?" she asked worriedly. "Could she have missed the plane?"

Before Danny could answer, a voice called out from behind them.

"Stephanie? Is that you?"

Stephanie whirled around to see a tall, pretty girl holding a carry-on suitcase and a canvas bag. She'd seen her walk out of the gate before and had admired her outfit—a tight black catsuit under a flowy sheer dress.

That couldn't possibly be Kyra, Stephanie thought in shock. *That girl is gorgeous! And she looks much older than thirteen.*

"Kyra?" Stephanie asked slowly.

The girl smiled an enormous smile and ran to Stephanie, throwing her arms around her.

"Betty! I thought that was you!" Kyra cried out. "Wow! Your hair got so long. Much longer than in the picture you sent me."

Stephanie knew she should say something, but she couldn't move or speak. She was in total shock. She managed to smile back, but she was just too stunned that this mature, beautiful girl with the sophisticated clothes and cool southern accent was the same girl she'd been writing to for the past three years.

"And you must be Stephanie's dad," Kyra said to Danny. "Hi! It's so nice to finally meet y'all." She yawned loudly. "Excuse me," she giggled, "but I'm so tired. That flight was the pits. This rude man sat next to me in the aisle seat and he slept the whole time. I couldn't even get up to go to the bathroom!"

Stephanie managed a laugh. "Y-You look great," she was finally able to say.

"I do?" Kyra asked, staring down at her dress. "I feel like a wrinkled mess. Can we stop in the ladies' room for a sec?"

Danny looked at his watch. "Of course. But make it quick, okay, girls? It's already pretty late and you have school tomorrow."

"No problem, Dad. C'mon, Kyra."

They left Kyra's luggage with Danny and headed for the ladies' room. Inside, Kyra splashed some water on her face and shook out her long, curly blond hair.

"Your perm looks awesome," Stephanie told her, reaching up to touch her own hair. "Maybe I should get one."

"You would look great with a perm, Steph," Kyra said. She reached into her pocket and pulled out a lipstick. Puckering, she put a glossy layer of red on her lips.

Stephanie's eyes widened. "Wow, you're allowed to wear lipstick?" she asked, incredulous.

Kyra shrugged. "Yeah, sure. No big deal."

Stephanie frowned. "I wish my father felt that way," she said. "He says no makeup until high school."

"Bummer," Kyra mumbled, blotting her lips with a tissue. "I always wear makeup, but not too much."

"You look great in makeup," Stephanie told her. "And that catsuit is way cool."

Kyra smiled. "It's my favorite outfit," she said.

Stephanie looked down at her own outfit—the outfit she had spent hours picking out—and suddenly felt like a six-year-old. How had she let Michelle convince her to wear these plain old baggy shorts and T-shirt?

"We'd better go," Stephanie finally said. "Dad's waiting."

As the girls piled into the Tanner van, Stephanie watched Kyra's every move. Kyra was so mature! And totally cool. Even the way she sat in the van with her legs crossed at the knees and her hands folded in her lap was cool. Stephanie suddenly felt lucky to have such a pretty, mature friend. She couldn't wait to bring Kyra to school and introduce her to everyone. She also couldn't wait to tell Kyra all the exciting things she had planned for her visit.

"On Saturday," Stephanie told her on the ride home, "we can tour downtown San Francisco. You know, like see the sights and stuff. And I had my uncle Jesse get two tickets for a Warriors game for Sunday night, so—"

"What's that?" Kyra asked with a yawn. "Baseball?"

Stephanie was caught by surprise. "Baseball? No, silly, it's basketball. The Golden State Warriors. You know, with Chris Webber and Tim Hardaway."

Kyra shrugged. "Never heard of 'em. But, uh, Steph, I was hoping maybe we could go into Berkeley one day and see all the hippies."

Stephanie made a face. "What for?" she asked.

"I don't know, I thought that would be cool." Kyra stretched her arms out in front of her and yawned again.

"Well, okay," Stephanie said apprehensively, "if you want to, we can go to Berkeley, I guess. Maybe on Sunday we can go to the mall with my friends Allie and Darcy. They're great, really, and they can't wait to meet—"

Stephanie stopped suddenly. Was Kyra snoring? She couldn't believe it.

"Kyra?" she asked softly.

"I think it's past Kyra's bedtime," Danny said. "Remember, there's a time difference, honey."

Kyra snored again. Her dad was right—she

was fast asleep. Stephanie leaned back in her seat and sighed. Who could sleep at a time like this? She gazed out the van window for the rest of the ride home.

It was late when Danny pulled into the driveway. The house was dark except for the front porch light.

Stephanie carried Kyra's bags up to her room and put them on Michelle's bed. It had taken one bribe after another to get Michelle to bunk with D.J. for Kyra's stay, but she had finally managed to do it by promising to french-braid Michelle's hair for an entire week.

Kyra rubbed her eyes and looked around Stephanie's room.

"Your house sure is nice," she said sleepily.

Stephanie smiled. "Come on! I'll give you the grand tour."

Kyra shook her head. "Maybe tomorrow, Steph. I'm so tired. It's two A.M. my time, you know. I'd better get some sleep."

"Oh, right, sure," Stephanie said. "I guess I'll just show you the bathroom, then. So you can get ready for bed."

"Thanks."

Stephanie led Kyra to the bathroom, then went back to her room and flopped onto her bed. She was really hoping Kyra would want to stay up late and talk. When she had sleepovers with Allie and Darcy, they usually stayed up until way after midnight, telling stories and jokes or just gossiping. And Stephanie was dying to ask Kyra about Brandon Fallow. She'd been thinking about asking Brandon to go with her to Skate for School night after all. Only she didn't have the guts to actually say the words to him. She was hoping Kyra would have some good advice.

When Kyra returned from the bathroom, Stephanie ran to brush her teeth. Maybe if she hurried, Kyra might change her mind and want to hang out a little before going to sleep. Stephanie brushed quickly, then raced back to her room, but when she got there, Kyra was fast asleep in Michelle's bed.

Stephanie sighed. *Well, we still have nine more nights together*, she reminded herself.

She got into bed and flicked off the light. She closed her eyes and fell asleep dreaming of the perfect roller-skating date with Brandon. They were holding hands and skating to Celine Dion's "The Power of Love." And in her dream Stephanie was wearing this totally hot black catsuit with a sheer dress that flowed gracefully behind her as she skated.

CHAPTER
4

◆ ◀ ◆ ◆

"But, Brandon," Stephanie said shyly, "I never knew you had a crush on me."

"I've had a crush on you ever since you were in sixth grade," Brandon replied.

"Well, now that we're going out, I guess you'll want me to wear your team jacket," Stephanie said happily.

"You bet! And we'll go Rollerblading together every Friday night, too," Brandon told her. "What do you think about that?" he whispered sweetly in her ear. "Stephanie? Stephanie? . . . Stephanie?"

Stephanie opened her eyes. It was dark and she wasn't exactly sure where she was.

"Stephanie?" a voice whispered again.

"Huh? Brandon?" Stephanie uttered in confusion.

Kyra giggled softly. "Stephanie, you've been dreaming! It's me, Kyra."

Stephanie sat up in bed and rubbed her eyes. "I . . . I . . . guess I *was* dreaming," she said sleepily.

"You thought I was Brandon!" Kyra laughed in a whisper. "Is he the guy you wrote me about?"

Stephanie nodded and yawned deeply. "Boy, am I tired! I can't believe it's time to get up already. I didn't even hear the alarm go off." She tried to focus on her alarm clock.

"Kyra!" she gasped. "It's four twenty-six in the morning."

"I know. I'm sorry for waking you," Kyra said, still whispering. "But I woke up and couldn't fall back to sleep. I just wanted to know if you had a nail file."

"A nail file?" Stephanie asked in disbelief. She still felt sort of loopy from having been woken up.

"Yeah, I broke a nail getting my bag out from

the overhead compartment on the plane last night."

Stephanie shook her head and yawned again. Begrudgingly, she pulled herself out of bed and went over to her dresser. Reaching into the top drawer, she took out an emery board. "Here," she said, yawning again.

"Thanks," Kyra whispered. "Now go back to sleep."

Stephanie walked back to her bed in a daze. She fell onto her pillow and closed her eyes. Just as she was about to drift off, a clicking noise disrupted her.

Click. Click. Click-click-click.

Stephanie sat up again. "Uh, Kyra, what's going on?"

"Oh!" Kyra whispered. "I woke you again, didn't I? I'm so sorry. It's just this dumb suitcase I have. The latch is stuck. I wanted to unpack, but I can't seem to get it open."

Stephanie let out a huge sigh of exhaustion. She got out of bed a second time and snatched the suitcase from Kyra. "Joey has the same suitcase," she said sleepily. "You have to jiggle it like this, pinch this part here, and, *voilà*, it's open." She handed the open bag to Kyra, then fell back onto her bed.

"Thanks, Stephanie!" Kyra said quietly. "Now go back to sleep. I won't wake you again. I promise."

Yeah, right, Stephanie grumbled in her mind. She mustered up a halfhearted smile, then buried her face in her pillow. *Kyra is certainly an early bird,* she thought to herself. *Not like me. I could sleep until noon every day if it weren't for school.*

When Kyra left the room to take a shower, Stephanie finally fell back asleep. She had almost drifted back to her wonderful dream date with Brandon, when all of a sudden she felt a blast of cold air. She pulled the covers up tighter and tried to doze off. But suddenly Stephanie felt drops of water on her face. *Is this a dream,* Stephanie wondered, *or am I in the middle of a rainstorm?*

With a jolt Stephanie bounced up from her pillow. To her surprise, she found Kyra standing at the foot of her bed, swinging her hair from right to left. Droplets of water were flying around the room.

"Go back to sleep," Kyra whispered loudly. "I'm just trying to dry my hair naturally in the fresh air."

"Fresh air?" Stephanie repeated, blinking in confusion.

"Now go back to sleep, Stephanie. Don't worry, I'll wake you when it's time to get up for school," Kyra said.

"I'm sure you will," Stephanie muttered under her breath. She flopped back onto her pillow and stared at the ceiling. It was no use. She might as well just get up. It didn't look as if she'd be able to get any more sleep that morning.

She lifted herself out of bed and dragged herself over to her closet to get her robe.

Kyra watched her. "Insomnia, huh?" she asked with a sympathetic look.

"You could say that," Stephanie mumbled. She pulled her robe off its hook in the closet and sluggishly shuffled to the bathroom.

When she finished showering, Stephanie headed back to her bedroom and stopped at the top of the stairs. There were a lot of voices coming from the kitchen below. She wondered what was going on. Her house was usually pretty noisy, but never at five-thirty in the morning.

Stephanie blow-dried her hair, then pulled on her favorite pair of jeans. Tucking in a crisp, white T-shirt, she topped off the outfit with the faded red denim vest D.J. had recently handed down to her. She studied herself in the mirror and decided it was going to be a great-outfit day. She tried to ignore the fact that her eyes were red and puffy from lack of sleep.

She brushed her hair one last time, then headed downstairs to investigate all the commotion.

In the kitchen Stephanie's entire family was seated around the table.

"What's everyone doing up?" she asked, still talking with a hoarse morning voice.

"Hey, Steph!" D.J. called out cheerfully. "Check it out! Kyra's making us all breakfast!"

Stephanie gazed into the kitchen, and sure enough, there was Kyra happily preparing food. Stephanie did a double take when she saw Kyra's outfit. Black leggings, a black shirt, black boots, and a black choker around her neck.

"Your friend is the greatest, Stephanie!" Joey

said, interrupting her thoughts. "She's making us an Atlanta breakfast specialty—rice cake cobbler!"

"Yeah, Stephanie," Michelle chimed in. "You can invite Kyra here anytime!"

Stephanie watched as her father sucked down one Georgia Peach Rice Cake after another.

"I thought you hated those things, Dad," Stephanie said, yawning.

"We *do* hate them," Michelle replied. "But Kyra makes them excellent!"

Kyra blushed. "No big deal, really. It's just a little yogurt and some fresh peaches. Why do you have so many bags of Georgia Peach Rice Cakes around?" she asked.

Everyone became silent suddenly and looked at Stephanie. She had made everybody promise to keep the contest a secret from Kyra.

"Oh, uh, they're all D.J.'s!" Stephanie blurted out.

D.J. gazed at her sister. "Mine?" she asked.

"Yes, *yours*," Stephanie repeated through clenched teeth. "Remember how you asked Dad to buy them for you because you love them so much?"

41

D.J. seemed confused at first, but then caught on. "Oh, right! Of course! They're mine! Boy, do I love those rice cakes!"

Stephanie glared at her sister's feeble attempt to lie and hoped Kyra hadn't noticed.

Kyra just shrugged and went back to mixing some crumbled cakes and yogurt in a big bowl. "Steph, sit down. I'm making a fresh batch for you."

Stephanie breathed a sigh of relief, then took her seat at the table. She watched as Nicky and Alex sat happily, munching away on rice cakes.

"Are those the same two kids who were building cities with those rice cakes yesterday?" she asked.

Becky laughed. "Can you believe it? They actually like them prepared this way."

"Steph," Danny said, "Kyra's been telling us all about herself. Did you know she was a vegetarian?"

"No, I didn't," Stephanie said in surprise. "Kyra, you never told me that."

"I guess I just forgot," Kyra said casually. "I decided to become one only a few months ago."

Michelle smiled proudly. "I know what a vega, a vetag . . ."

"A vegetarian," Danny said.

"Right, a vegetarian. I know what a vegetarian is. It's when you don't eat hot dogs."

"That's right, Michelle," Kyra answered from behind the stove. "But not just hot dogs. No hamburgers, no steak, no chicken, no meat at all."

"How come you're a veta . . . a vega . . . How come you don't eat meat?" Michelle asked.

"Because innocent animals are killed to make those foods, and besides, they're not as healthy for you as vegetables are."

Michelle looked confused. "What animals are hamburgers?"

"Cows," Kyra told her.

"Oh, yuck!" Michelle exclaimed. "No more hamburgers for me!" she proclaimed. Then suddenly her face clouded over and she swallowed hard. She gazed at her father nervously. "If hamburgers are dead cows," she said, "does that mean hot dogs are . . . *dead dogs?*" she asked, her voice trembling.

Comet, the family dog, barked.

Uncle Jesse tried not to laugh. "No, silly," he said. "Hot dogs are not dogs!" He lifted her up.

"Then what are hot dogs?" she asked him.

Jesse smiled. "Well, Michelle, hot dogs are . . . they're . . . uh, actually I'm not exactly sure what hot dogs are," he said, putting Michelle back down. "Cows, maybe, horses, I guess, and—"

"Okay!" Danny interrupted loudly, seeing the horrified look on Michelle's face. "Michelle, honey, how would you like it if I drove you to school today?"

Michelle's expression changed instantly. "Yeah!" she exclaimed. "Can we talk about where hot dogs come from?" she asked.

"Sure, no problem," Danny replied uneasily. "Steph, do you and Kyra want a ride today, too?"

Stephanie didn't answer.

"Steph?"

Again she didn't answer.

"Steph? Honey? *Stephanie!*"

Startled, Stephanie jumped in her seat, accidentally elbowing her cereal bowl and sending the bowl, the milk, and the rice cake cobbler flying all over the place. "What? What?" she asked in confusion.

Nicky and Alex giggled. Michelle joined in.

"Steph, were you sleeping?" D.J. asked.

"No, I was not sleeping!" Stephanie said defensively. "I was thinking."

"Yeah, right," D.J. said with a laugh. "With your eyes closed."

"What did you say, Dad?" Stephanie asked, ignoring her sister.

"I asked if you and Kyra wanted a ride to school today. After you clean up that mess, that is."

"Uh, no, Dad. We'll take the bus. I promised to meet Allie and Darcy." Stephanie rubbed her eyes and yawned sleepily. "Wait!" she shouted suddenly. "I almost forgot! Don't anybody leave yet! I need sponsors for Skate for School!"

"Skate for who?" Joey asked.

"Skate for School," Stephanie repeated. "It's like a walk-a-thon, except it's a skate-a-thon, where you get people to donate money for every hour you skate. All the money goes for school things like new computers and stuff. It's next

Friday night at the Bay City Rink. Kyra and I are going to skate the longest and raise the most money for school!" She smiled in Kyra's direction.

Kyra stopped chewing. "Ha!" she laughed loudly. "Me? On Rollerblades? What, are you kidding?"

Stephanie's mouth fell open. "You . . . you don't Rollerblade, Kyra?" she asked in disbelief.

Kyra shook her head. "Stephanie, I thought you knew I was a total klutz on skates! I can't even *look* at a pair without falling down."

"Uh, no, I didn't know that," Stephanie said quietly. "You'll still come, though, right?"

Kyra shrugged. "Sure, I guess. But I'm *not* putting on skates. And since when do *you* like Rollerblading?" she asked.

Stephanie gazed at Kyra in amazement. "Are you joking? I've been Rollerblading for years. I skate every single weekend! I love it!"

"Well, not me," Kyra said, finishing her breakfast.

How could Kyra not know about her love for skating? Stephanie wondered. She must have mentioned it in one of her letters.

"But you'll still come?" Stephanie asked again.

"Sure."

Stephanie sighed, then held up her sponsor sheet. "So who's going to sponsor me? Dad? Joey?"

"Dad? Joey?" Uncle Jesse repeated. "What am I? Chopped liver?"

"Please, Jess," Joey joked, "not in front of the vegetarian."

"Whoops, sorry, Kyra," Jesse said. "But, Stephanie, don't you want me to sponsor you? You know I'd do anything to further the education of our youth. I mean, someday Nicky and Alex will be your age, and, well, what if there's no money in the budget for textbooks? Or computers? Or—" he stopped in mid-sentence when he looked in his wallet.

"That's funny," he said, scratching his head. "I was sure I put some cash in here last night." He shrugged. "Well, can I give you money tomorrow, Steph?"

"Uncle Jesse," Stephanie said, "you're *already* sponsoring me."

"I am?"

"Uh-huh. Nicky and Alex gave me money last night."

Jesse eyed his twin boys suspiciously. "They did, eh? And would they, by chance, have sponsored you for thirty-four dollars"—he stopped to check his pockets—"and sixty-two cents?"

Stephanie looked at her sponsor sheet. "Yup. Exactly," she said.

Jesse scooped up both twins at once and headed for the attic. "Let's go, Bonnie and Clyde. I'm putting an end to your life of crime before your fourth birthday."

Stephanie helped clear the table, then turned to Kyra. "We should get going," she said. "I usually meet my friends at the bus stop at the corner."

"Great! Let's go!" Kyra stopped at the mirror by the door and opened her bag. She reached in and pulled out a black beret, then put it on her head.

Stephanie almost choked. "Uh, are you planning on wearing that hat to school?" she asked uneasily.

Kyra stopped walking and stared at Stephanie. "Yes. Why? Does it look bad?" she asked.

"Oh, no," Stephanie assured her, "it looks

great on you. It's just that, well, no one at school wears berets."

Kyra shrugged. "Well, lots of kids in my school wear them."

There was an uncomfortable silence.

"Yeah, okay, no problem," Stephanie finally said, opening the front door. She tried to sound casual, but deep down she felt totally nervous. What were her friends going to say when they saw Kyra's strange outfit?

CHAPTER
5

◆ ◄ ◆ ◆

Stephanie couldn't have been more wrong about Kyra's outfit. Her friends thought it was awesome. Darcy and Allie even asked to try on Kyra's beret.

In fact, not only was Kyra's outfit a huge hit at school, Kyra herself was the major talk of the school by lunchtime. In the cafeteria a crowd of kids gathered around Stephanie's table, asking Kyra all sorts of questions about Atlanta.

Stephanie was completely thrilled. After all, Kyra was *her* best friend.

When the crowd of kids left, it was just Stephanie, Kyra, Allie, and Darcy, and pretty soon the talk turned to Friday night and Skate for School.

"Check this out!" Darcy exclaimed in a loud whisper. "I heard that Dana Michaelson asked Keith Cavanaugh to go with her!"

"Which one is Keith?" Kyra asked.

"He's the one we passed in the hall before who was talking to Corey Altman," Allie told her.

"With the brownish hair?" Kyra asked.

"That's him," Darcy said.

"Wow," Stephanie said with a yawn. "I can't believe Dana got up the nerve to ask him."

"Lots of girls have dates," Darcy pointed out.

"Big deal," Allie said. "We'll have fun going together. Just the four of us. We don't need dates. Unless, of course, Steph decides to ask Brandon!"

Stephanie turned red. "I can't ask Brandon!" she exclaimed. "Remember that time I had to tell him he dropped his notebook in the hall-way? I practically fainted! How could I just go up to him and say, 'Hey, Brandon, wanna go to Skate for School with me?' I'd pass out for sure!"

"Then maybe Brandon can give you mouth-to-mouth resuscitation!" Darcy joked.

Everyone laughed. "Now, there's an idea!" Stephanie declared dreamily. "But seriously. I'll never have the guts to ask Brandon anything."

"So what crazy plans do y'all have for tonight?" Kyra asked, her eyes shining with excitement.

Darcy and Allie looked at each other, then shrugged. "Uh, nothing, really," Darcy said.

"We thought you and Stephanie had plans already," Allie added.

Kyra looked at Stephanie. "Really? What are we doing tonight?" she asked.

Stephanie smiled. "Tonight," she announced happily, "my dad's taking us to Wo Hop's!"

Darcy's and Allie's eyes widened in excitement. "Excellent!" Darcy cried.

Kyra made a face. "What's Wo Hop's?" she asked, scrunching up her nose.

"Only the best Chinese food in San Francisco," Stephanie proclaimed.

Kyra's top lip curled in disgust. "Chinese?" she asked.

"Yeah, why?" Stephanie asked.

"Well, I thought you knew, Stephanie. I don't really like Chinese food."

Stephanie's heart sank. Kyra didn't like Chinese? How could that be? Chinese food was Stephanie's absolute favorite food in the world.

"Oh, uh, well, I guess we can go somewhere else," Stephanie said hesitantly. "I suppose my dad can cancel our reservations and—"

"Well, if it's all planned and everything," Kyra said, "I mean, I'll go. I'm sure I can find *something* to eat there."

After that it got uncomfortably quiet. "So, uh, I'm thinking of getting a perm," Stephanie said, breaking the awkward silence.

Allie's eyes widened. "No way!" she said.

Stephanie nodded. "Really. Kyra thinks I'd look good with curly hair. Right, Kyra?"

"Uh-huh," Kyra replied, taking out her lipstick.

Stephanie, Allie, and Darcy watched in envy as Kyra put Ruby Red on her lips.

Suddenly Allie gasped. "Don't look now," she whispered excitedly, "but Brandon Fallow is on his way over here!"

Naturally Stephanie, Darcy, and Kyra all looked up, anyway, just in time for Brandon to say, "Hey."

Stephanie managed to say hello back, but her voice came out sounding funny. *Thank heaven I'm having a good-outfit day* was all she could think.

Brandon smiled. "Hey, Stephanie. My friend Paul, from your English class, told me you had a friend visiting you from Atlanta."

Stephanie was still in a fog, shocked that Brandon had actually said her name. That was the first time she'd heard him say it so casually, as if they were great friends. *Hey, Stephanie* was what he'd said. She sighed. She loved the way he'd said it.

Allie nudged her.

"Oh, right," Stephanie said, "I do. I mean, she is. I mean, this is Kyra Jourdan. Kyra, this is Brandon Fallow."

"Hi, Kyra," Brandon said. "You know, I'm from Atlanta, too."

Stephanie's eyes widened. *I never knew that*, she thought to herself. Her heart jumped. Now she and Brandon both had something in common—Atlanta. He was from there and one of Stephanie's best friends was, too.

"You are?" Kyra asked excitedly. "Where?"

"Well, I lived in White Water for six years while my dad worked for Coca-Cola."

"Oh, sure, I know that neighborhood," Kyra said, nodding. "They have that cool movie complex there."

"That's right!" Brandon exclaimed. "I used to love that place!"

"My friends and I go there all the time," Kyra said. "And to that great park—"

"Shelby Lake!" Brandon declared. "I played Little League in that park."

Stephanie was beaming. Her heart thumped faster than it ever had. She heard the bell ring for class, but she couldn't move. *Brandon Fallow is standing two feet away from me,* she thought breathlessly, *talking to one of my best friends. He said my name and now we're practically hanging out together!*

Allie had to nudge her again and bring her back to reality. "Steph, we have math, remember?"

Stephanie shot Allie a look. "Of course I

remember," she said. Only she didn't want the moment to end. She wished she could stand in the cafeteria for another few hours, talking to Brandon. She couldn't believe she had to leave. Darn math! It was ruining her life. Finally she turned to Kyra and Brandon.

"Kyra, we really ought to go," she said.

"Sure," Kyra said.

"Uh, bye, Brandon," Stephanie said, flashing what she hoped was her very best smile.

"Bye, Stephanie," he replied. "See you later. And nice meeting you, Kyra."

Stephanie stared after him as he joined his friends across the cafeteria. "Did you hear what he said?" she asked dreamily. " 'Bye, Stephanie. See you later.' " She sighed.

"So that's the famous Brandon," Kyra said with a smile. "The guy of your dreams, so to speak."

Stephanie blushed. "Yup. Isn't he adorable?"

Kyra nodded. "Totally! He reminds me of—"

Darcy interrupted anxiously. "Guys! Math . . . remember?"

Stephanie made a face. "Right. Math. Like

I'll really be able to concentrate on geometry today."

Kyra laughed. "Oh, well, I guess you'll just have to fall asleep in class and get into dream mode so you can see Brandon!"

"It wouldn't be the first time," Stephanie joked as they walked to class.

CHAPTER
6

Stephanie sat on her bed, watching Kyra polish her fingernails. She looked at her watch for the tenth time, then back to Kyra, who was blowing on her fingers and shaking her hands out in front of her.

"Kyra, are they almost dry?" she asked impatiently. "We're leaving for Wo Hop's any minute. You promised to help me pick out something to wear."

Kyra blew on her nails again. "Almost," she said. "But really, Stephanie, why don't you just wear what you have on? We're only going out to dinner."

Stephanie frowned and looked at her boring T-shirt and jeans. Then she looked at Kyra's outfit—she was wearing one of those holey sweaters with a bodysuit underneath, biker shorts, and clunky clogs. She looked so sophisticated.

"I look like a seventh grader," Stephanie groaned unhappily.

"Steph, you *are* a seventh grader."

Stephanie got up from her bed and took a pair of Keds from the closet. What she'd really been hoping was that Kyra would offer to lend her one of her outfits. She thought she'd hinted at it enough, but Kyra had obviously not taken the cue. Even after Stephanie went so far as to say, "Kyra, you have the coolest clothes. I wonder how they'd look on me." She sighed loudly, then tied her sneakers.

Downstairs, everyone was getting ready to leave. Jesse and Becky were chasing after the twins with sweatshirts, Danny and D.J. were arguing, and Michelle was waiting by the door, holding her red chopsticks—an eighth-birthday gift from Stephanie.

"We can't all fit in the van, Dad," D.J. said. "I'll drive Stephanie and Kyra in the station wagon."

"What about me?" Michelle asked.

"And Michelle," D.J. added.

Danny shook his head. "No, D.J.," he said calmly. "I think it's best if Jesse takes Becky and the twins in the wagon and the rest of us go in the van."

D.J. sulked.

So did Jesse. "I don't feel like driving," he complained. "My tummy hurts."

"Tummy hurts!" Nicky repeated. "Tummy hurts!"

Becky smiled gently. "No, sweetie, not *your* tummy. Daddy's tummy hurts." She gazed at her husband. "You know, Jess, you do look a little green."

"I do?" Jesse asked, rushing to the mirror to see his reflection. "You're right," he gasped. "I am green." Then he gasped even louder. "Even worse!" he cried, staring in the mirror. "I see a gray hair!"

Becky rolled her eyes. "Never mind, Jesse. If you're just faking it to get out of going out for dinner, you can forget it. We're going!"

Jesse frowned. "But my tummy hurts," he moaned again.

"Come on, Dad," D.J. wailed again. "Please? I'll be real careful. I promise."

Danny sighed loudly. "Okay, okay! Let's just go already."

"Finally," Michelle announced. "Wo Hop's, here we come."

"Wo Hop's! Wo Hop's!" the boys chanted as they marched out the door.

Stephanie, Kyra, D.J., and Michelle sat in the entryway to Wo Hop's. Stephanie sighed loudly and brushed Michelle's hair as her younger sister laid with her head in Stephanie's lap. Stephanie checked her watch again.

Finally, everyone else arrived. Danny and Joey were arguing, and Jesse and Becky each held a sleeping twin.

"You shouldn't have told the policeman that your van was so spotless," Joey said. "I don't know why you felt you had to show him the trunk, either. What were you thinking?"

"I don't know!" Danny replied. "I was all nervous about getting a ticket. I thought if I showed him how clean we kept the van, he'd reconsider."

61

Joey just shook his head. "I can't believe it," he muttered under his breath. "A ticket for driving too *slow*."

"Dad, can we eat already?" Michelle asked, yawning. "I'm starving."

"Me, too," Stephanie said.

Danny sighed and stared at his hungry daughters. "Of course, Michelle," he said gently. "Let's get a table."

"We don't have our reservation anymore," Stephanie pointed out. "It was for six-thirty, and now it's seven-thirty."

Luckily there was a party of ten just leaving, and pretty soon they were all seated around a big table, holding menus.

"Look, Kyra, we can share the moo shu pork," Stephanie said, pointing to the menu. "You eat the moo shu and I'll eat the pork."

Kyra made a face. "No way! The moo shu is cooked with the pork. Yuck."

"What about shrimps in garlic sauce," D.J. suggested.

Kyra shook her head. "No, I don't eat seafood."

"You can have some of my spareribs," Michelle offered happily. "It's not a cow, right?"

"Michelle, spareribs aren't from cows, they're from pigs," Kyra said.

Michelle's eyes widened. "Pigs?" she asked.

Kyra nodded.

"Like Porky, Miss Piggy, and the Three Little," Stephanie told her.

Michelle thought for a moment, then made an announcement.

"I've decided to become a veterinarian!" she declared.

"You mean a vegetarian," Stephanie corrected her.

"Right," Michelle said.

"So, Kyra, how did you like Stephanie's school today?" Danny asked.

"Okay, I guess," she replied. "School is school, you know."

Stephanie was confused. Kyra had said she'd had a great time.

"Was it much different from your school in Atlanta?" D.J. asked.

"Definitely," Kyra said. "Everybody in my school really dresses up. It isn't so casual."

Stephanie stared down at her plate, wondering if Kyra was referring to her T-shirt and jeans.

"Also, I usually have rehearsals after school, so I don't get home until much later."

"Rehearsals?" Stephanie asked. "For what?"

Kyra stared at Stephanie in surprise. "For the play, of course," she said. "I told you I got the lead in our spring play, *Barefoot in the Park.*"

Stephanie's mouth fell open. "No! You didn't tell me that. You got the lead?"

Kyra nodded.

"That's great, Kyra," Joey told her. "I was in that play in high school."

Stephanie sat back in her chair in shock. How could Kyra have forgotten to tell her about something as important as that? She was beginning to think there was a lot she didn't know about Kyra Jourdan.

Kyra talked on and on about the play, and by the time the food came, she and Joey were practically acting the whole thing out. Stephanie was feeling very left out.

Becky took one look at her food, then

dropped her head on the table and grimaced in pain.

"Oooh, my stomach," she wailed, bolting up from the table. She ran to the ladies' room.

"Uncle Jesse, aren't you going to go after her?" D.J. asked.

Jesse gazed up at everyone with a glassy look in his eyes. "You know, come to think of it," he said queasily, "I'm not feeling so hot myself. Steph, keep an eye on the twins, will ya?" A second later he ran to the men's room.

"Tummy hurts, too!" Nicky shouted.

"Me, too!" Alex added, laughing.

Stephanie moved over to sit with the boys, who kept shouting "Tummy! Tummy!" and throwing noodles and rice at each other.

"Nicky! Alex! Stop that," Stephanie said.

"Daddy, I'm still hungry," Michelle cried.

"Well, you didn't eat anything except rice, Michelle," Danny pointed out. "Just have a bite of Aunt Becky's Peking duck. She won't be eating any more, I'm sure."

"Duck?" Michelle asked in horror. "You mean like Daffy? And Donald?"

Danny put his head in his hands. "What a night this is turning out to be," he said helplessly.

Across the table Stephanie was covered from head to toe with fried rice. "You can say that again, Dad."

Pretty soon Jesse and Becky came back to the table. "We're leaving," Jesse announced. "I think Becky and I ate too many of those spicy rice cake tamales this afternoon. We'll take the boys home in the station wagon. Okay, D.J.?"

"No problem, Uncle Jesse," D.J. said. "We'll ride home in the van. With Dad." She smiled halfheartedly at her father.

After Jesse and Becky left, the table grew quiet.

"My boyfriend's family back home has a Winnebago trailer," Kyra announced, breaking the silence. "It's the coolest. They drive all over the country in it."

Stephanie felt her heart stop. *Boyfriend? Did Kyra just say she had a boyfriend?*

"Those are pretty cool," Joey said. "I've always wanted a big camper like that. Stephanie, wouldn't having a camper be awesome?"

Stephanie didn't answer.

"Stephanie?" Joey asked again.

"Kyra, you didn't tell me you had a boyfriend," Stephanie said.

"Sure I did!" Kyra said. "In my last letter. I must have told you about Scott."

"The guy from homeroom?" Stephanie asked.

Kyra smiled. "No, that was Tom Westman. He never asked me out. I didn't tell you about Scott Zacharin? He's in the play with me."

Stephanie shook her head in shock. She thought she and Kyra told each other everything—especially something as important as a new boyfriend. But here she was, hearing it for the first time with her family.

Kyra got a dreamy look in her eyes. "Scott's the best," she gushed. "He's so cute and so sweet. And he's a really good actor, too. We're going to take acting lessons together."

"That's great, Kyra," D.J. said.

Stephanie shot a look at her sister. Great? What was so great about it? Here Kyra had a boyfriend for all this time and had never bothered to tell her best friend about it. What was so great about that?

"Dad, when are we going home?" Stephanie asked.

"I'm getting the check right now," Danny told her.

Excellent, Stephanie thought. She was hoping to put an end to this night. It hadn't exactly turned out like she'd hoped.

"Hey! I have a great idea!" D.J. suddenly announced. "Let's take Kyra to Putt Putt!"

Michelle jumped out of her seat. "Oh, Dad, can we? Huh? Can we?"

Stephanie groaned. "Putt Putt?" she said in disgust. "I don't think Kyra wants to play miniature golf. Can't we just go home?" She looked pleadingly at Danny.

"No, I love miniature golf!" Kyra declared. "Come on, Stephanie, let's go. It'll be fun."

Stephanie groaned quietly. She hated miniature golf. But she saw the excitement on Kyra's face. "Sure," she said, trying to sound enthusiastic. "Putt Putt sounds like fun."

It was eleven-thirty when they got home from Putt Putt. Stephanie was so irritated, she went straight to her room and closed the door behind her. She couldn't believe how much worse the night had become.

Kyra had spent the entire evening talking and laughing with D.J.—she'd barely said a word to Stephanie except for "It's your shot, Stephanie." And to top it all off, Kyra and D.J. swapped boyfriend stories the whole time, leaving Stephanie out completely.

A few minutes later there was a knock on Stephanie's door. "Hey, Steph, it's me. Can I come in?"

Stephanie frowned. Kyra was the last person she felt like seeing right now.

"Uh-huh," she answered flatly.

Kyra opened the door and saw Stephanie lying on her bed. "That was fun, huh?" she asked.

"Yeah, right," Stephanie mumbled.

Kyra yawned. "I think I'm going to turn in, okay? I still have jet lag and I'm feeling kind of spacey. It's almost three o'clock my time, you know."

Stephanie hid her face and rolled her eyes. "I know, I know," she said. She watched as Kyra got ready for bed. By the time Stephanie came back from brushing her teeth, Kyra was already out cold.

"It figures," Stephanie muttered quietly. *Well, there's always tomorrow,* she thought to herself as she turned off the light. *I have the whole day planned for just the two of us. Maybe things will be better when it's just Kyra and me.*

CHAPTER
7

◆ ◀ ◆ ◆

"My whole day is ruined!" Stephanie cried. "Ruined!" It was Saturday morning, and she stood over D.J.'s bed, shaking her older sister awake.

"Stephanie, just chill out," D.J. said sleepily. She rubbed her eyes and sat up in bed.

"But, Deej, it's almost ten o'clock," Stephanie wailed. "We were supposed to leave for the city an hour ago."

D.J. sighed. "Well, when did Kyra say she would be back?" she asked.

"She didn't," Stephanie replied. "Now the whole day is shot. We'll never fit everything in!"

71

"Where did Kyra go, anyway?" Michelle asked, sitting up on her foldaway bed.

Stephanie sat next to D.J.'s pillow. "She went jogging. She left at 5:57 this morning."

"How do you know that?" D.J. asked.

"Because I was up!" Stephanie exclaimed.

"What were you doing up so early on a Saturday morning?" D.J. asked.

Stephanie hopped off the bed and paced anxiously back and forth. "What was I doing up?" she asked in exasperation. "You want to know what I was doing up? I'll tell you what I was doing up! Kyra needed some toothpaste. Then Kyra needed a sweatband. Then Kyra woke me for directions to the park. Then Kyra needed a hair scrunchie! That's what I was doing up at six o'clock on a Saturday morning. Searching the bottom of my closet for a hair scrunchie!"

"Steph, calm down," D.J. said. "I swear, you are out of control this morning. It's no big deal if you don't get to see every inch of San Francisco with Kyra."

"But I made all these plans and everything," Stephanie sulked.

"Something else is bothering you, Steph. I can tell," D.J. said knowingly.

"Me, too," Michelle chimed in.

Stephanie walked to the window and peered down the street, hoping to see Kyra. When she didn't, she went back to D.J.'s bed and sat down.

"Steph, what is it?" D.J. asked.

Stephanie sighed. "Okay, here's the deal," she said. "But you have to keep it a secret."

"Done," D.J. said.

"Yeah, done," Michelle added.

"I mean it, Michelle! I'm talking total secrecy, okay?"

Michelle pretended to zip her mouth shut.

Stephanie took a deep breath. "I thought things would be different with Kyra," she explained. "I thought we were really, really close. I thought we were practically twins. I mean, we always wrote to each other about how cool it was that we were so much alike and how we liked the same exact things. But now everything is so different. We're nothing alike. And I feel like I don't know anything about her!"

"But you must know something," D.J. said. "You've been writing to each other for three years."

"I know!" Stephanie exclaimed. "I thought I did. But I don't know her at all. She never told me about getting the lead in her school play, or about becoming a vegetarian, or even about her boyfriend! Aren't friends supposed to tell each other those things?"

"I tell Cassie and Lee everything," Michelle commented.

"Yeah, but you see them every day," D.J. pointed out. "Stephanie, you have a long-distance relationship with Kyra. It's much different than a regular friendship. There isn't enough room to tell somebody everything in a letter. You need to have a couple of real heart-to-heart talks and spend some time together in order to get to know someone. Kyra's been here only one day. Give it some more time."

"I know it's been only one day," Stephanie said. "But even so, Kyra and I haven't spent one single second together alone!"

"Really?" D.J. asked.

"Well, not counting the ladies' room at the airport, no. We haven't talked at all."

D.J. shook her head in sympathy. "All I can say, Steph, is give it some more time. You'll have all day today together. Just the two of you."

Stephanie got up and went back to the window. "Yeah, I guess you're right," she said softly. "I was thinking—wait! There she is!" Stephanie flung the window open.

"Yo! Kyra! Up here!" She turned to her sisters. "*Now* we can finally have some time alone together," she said happily. "I'm going to make sure we fill every minute with exciting things. Look out, San Francisco—we're going to paint the town red."

Michelle made a face. "Huh? Even the grass and the trees?"

"It's just an expression, Michelle," Stephanie said. "It means we're going to see and do everything in town. And we're going to have the time of our lives!"

A minute later Kyra poked her head into D.J.'s room. "Hey, guys," she said, a little out of breath. "It's beautiful out. This San Francisco air is just the best. I must have run twenty miles."

"Where did you go?" Stephanie asked.

"All over," Kyra said. "I jogged across the park. To the boathouse, the duck pond, the playground, and around the lake."

"Wow," Michelle said. "You painted that park red, huh?"

"I what?" Kyra asked, raising an eyebrow.

"Never mind her," Stephanie butted in. "You should hurry up and get changed. We have to leave for the city soon if we want to get all the sights in."

Kyra bit her bottom lip. "Uh, about sight-seeing today, Steph," she said hesitantly, "I'm kind of exhausted from the run. Maybe we could hang around here today, instead? We can go sight-seeing tomorrow."

Stephanie felt a lump form in her throat. *Hang around here?* she thought in dismay. *How boring!* She stared down at the floor. "Well, if that's what you want—" she mumbled.

"Great!" Kyra said, exhaling. "I knew you would understand, Steph. Thanks. I'm going to hit the shower now. See you in a bit."

When she was gone, Stephanie gazed at her sisters. "You see?"

"Just be a little patient," D.J. reminded her.

Stephanie tapped her pencil on her desk and rolled her eyes. She couldn't believe what she'd been listening to for the past two and a half hours. Michelle and Kyra were sitting on the floor of her room, looking at Michelle's zillion-page sticker collection. Michelle insisted on explaining each and every sticker.

"And Joey bought me this unicorn sticker last year when he went to Los Angeles," Michelle told Kyra. "See? It's made out of this stuff called Mylar and you can see your reflection in it."

Stephanie rolled her eyes again, then looked at her watch.

"That's pretty cool," Kyra said. "Where's this one from?" she asked, pointing to a big polar bear ballerina in a shiny pink tutu.

Michelle smiled. "That's my favorite sticker," she said. "D.J. and Stephanie gave it to me for my first ballet recital." She looked up and smiled at Stephanie.

Stephanie flashed her a quick smile, then stood up impatiently. "So, Kyra, do you want to go now?"

"Go where?" Kyra asked.

"To the grocery store, remember? Dad asked if we could pick up some cheese for the rice cake pizza dinner he's making."

Kyra grimaced. "Oh, I thought you went already."

"No, I was waiting for you," Stephanie said. "I thought you would want to take a walk with me. Maybe we can talk or something."

Kyra shrugged. "Sure. Let me get my hat."

Stephanie smiled. Finally! She and Kyra were going to spend some time alone.

Downstairs, Stephanie and Kyra were almost out the door when D.J. called to them from the sofa.

"Where are you two headed?" she asked.

"To the store, for Dad," Stephanie replied.

"Wanna come with us?" Kyra asked.

Stephanie glared at her sister.

"Oh, no, that's okay," D.J. answered, taking Stephanie's hint. "You guys go. You probably have a lot of catching up to do."

Kyra laughed. "Don't be silly, D.J.," she said. "We'd love you to come! Right, Stephanie?"

Stephanie managed a smile. "Right! Sure! Of course we would, Deej," she said, trying to sound convincing.

Unfortunately, it worked.

D.J. put down her magazine. "Really? Well, in

that case, I'd love to come. I need some conditioner, anyway." She ran up to her room to get money.

When she was gone, Kyra smiled at Stephanie. "You have such a great family," she said. "I wish I had sisters."

Stephanie smiled back. *You can have mine*, she thought to herself.

D.J. came running down the steps with her purse. "I'll treat you guys to some ice cream, too." She glanced at Stephanie. "Okay?"

"Yeah. No problem," Stephanie replied. She couldn't believe D.J. was coming with them. Hadn't her sister heard a word she'd said that morning?

"You just have to taste this great frozen dessert from the takeout counter," D.J. told Kyra as they walked. "They have the most incredible frozen tofu, right, Steph?"

Stephanie was silent. "Oh, were you talking to me?" she asked with a hint of sarcasm.

D.J. made a face. "Of course I'm talking to you."

"Well, I wouldn't know," Stephanie replied. "I hate tofu. I'd rather have real ice cream any day."

D.J. smirked. "That's because you've never had to watch your weight like the rest of us."

Kyra nodded in agreement. "Yeah, I wish I were as thin as you, Stephanie. Unfortunately I have a passion for sweets."

Stephanie looked at Kyra's gorgeous figure. "Kyra, you *are* thin."

"Now I am," Kyra answered, "but it's not easy for me to stay thin. I used to be very overweight, you know."

"You were?" Stephanie asked. "When?"

"Last year," Kyra answered. "I lost a ton of weight last year. Didn't I write you about it?"

"No," Stephanie answered.

"Hmmm, I thought I did. Anyway, that's one of the reasons I've recently become a vegetarian. Not only am I saving animals' lives, I'm trying to keep my weight down. So far it's working."

"Well, you'll just love this no-fat frozen tofu," D.J. told her.

"I can't wait to try it," Kyra said with a smile. "Scott eats healthy foods like that all the time. He eats only organically grown vegetables. Did I tell you how he took me to a farm on our first date?"

Stephanie shook her head. She was beginning to wonder what Kyra *had* told her in the past three years of letter writing.

Kyra giggled. "Oh, it was so romantic! We walked through a cornfield together and had a picnic in a barn!"

Stephanie scrunched up her nose. "A barn? With horses? Sounds *real* romantic," she joked.

Kyra sighed. "Sometimes romance isn't all candlelit dinners and walking along the beach, Stephanie. If you had a boyfriend, you'd understand."

Stephanie stopped dead in her tracks. She felt as if she'd just been slapped in the face.

Kyra's face turned red immediately. "I, uh, didn't mean that the way it came out, Stephanie. Really. I just meant—"

Stephanie kept walking. "Never mind, Kyra."

"No, really, Stephanie. That was so rude of me to say. It came out all wrong. I'm really sorry."

They walked the rest of the way in uncomfortable silence with D.J. desperately trying to make conversation. By the time they got to the store, Stephanie was glad when Kyra and D.J. left her alone to go find the frozen tofu.

When they were gone, Stephanie went to get the cheese. She couldn't believe Kyra had been so mean to her. How rude! Kyra's visit was turning out to be one surprise after another.

"Where did you guys go?" Michelle asked them when they returned.

"To the store for Dad," Stephanie answered her, tossing the cheese into the refrigerator. "I'll be up in my room if anyone needs me."

In her room Stephanie pulled her diary out from its secret hiding place beneath the carpet in her closet and fell into bed.

Saturday, March 26, she wrote. *Kyra's second day here.* She looked up from her diary and chewed on the tip of her pen.

I wish it were her last.

CHAPTER
8

◆ ◀ ◆ ◆

In gym class on Monday morning, Stephanie changed into her shorts and T-shirt slowly, waiting for Allie and Darcy. She'd dropped Kyra off at the library, then rushed to the girls' locker room. She couldn't wait to see Allie and Darcy.

Darcy arrived first.

"Close your eyes!" Darcy said with a grin. Her hands were behind her back.

"What for?" Stephanie asked grumpily.

"Ta-da!" Darcy called out, bringing her hands in front of her. She held out a bunch of Georgia Peach Rice Cakes contest entry forms.

Stephanie scoffed, then pointed to the trash

can. "You can put them in there," she said, pulling on her sweat socks.

Darcy seemed confused. "But—" she began.

Allie skipped in happily, cutting her off. "Hey, you two! What's up?" She smiled at Stephanie and opened her locker. "So, how did the big weekend go?"

"You wouldn't believe the weekend I had," Stephanie said, searching her locker for her sneakers.

Allie smiled. "Fun, huh?"

Stephanie's face fell. "Fun? Are you kidding? It was probably the worst weekend of my entire life!"

Darcy slipped into her shorts. "Why? What happened?" she asked.

Stephanie bent down to tie her sneakers. "Where do I begin?" she asked. "Kyra and I aren't clicking. At all."

Allie's eyes widened. "What are you talking about, Stephanie? I thought you said you two were so much alike."

"Ha!" Stephanie scoffed. "Boy, was I wrong! Not only aren't we anything alike, we're practically exact opposites! Kyra might as well be from Mars."

"Oh, come on, Steph, it can't be that bad," Darcy said.

"Really? Well, listen to this," Stephanie told them. "We went to Wo Hop's on Friday night, right? Well, we were all sitting there, having dinner, when Kyra started telling my entire family about her boyfriend, Scott."

"Wait a sec," Allie interrupted. "You didn't tell us that Kyra had a boyfriend."

"I know!" Stephanie exclaimed. "That's because Kyra never told *me!*"

"She never told you that?" Allie asked in disbelief. "But that's major big-time information."

Darcy's eyes narrowed. "How long have they been going out?" she asked.

"Long enough to have romantic picnics with horses," Stephanie muttered.

"Huh?" they asked.

"A long time," Stephanie said. "Three weeks. Now all she does is talk to D.J. about Scott and how much in love they are and all the romantic things she and Scott do. Meanwhile, she and I didn't get a single second to ourselves all weekend. Can you believe it?"

"What about your sight-seeing plans?" Allie asked.

"Oh, Kyra didn't *feel* like going sight-seeing this weekend," Stephanie replied.

"But you had such a great two days planned," Darcy said. "Fisherman's Wharf, the Ghirardelli chocolate factory, the trolley ride—"

"We didn't do any of it," Stephanie said. "Not one single thing."

"Then what *did* you do?" Allie asked.

"What did we do? I'll tell you what we did. We hung around the house all weekend!" Stephanie exclaimed.

Allie and Darcy both made faces. "Yuck!" Darcy said.

"Really?" Allie asked. "All weekend?"

Stephanie nodded. "Yup. That's what Kyra wanted to do. She wanted to sit in my room and look at Michelle's stickers. She wanted to watch television with my dad and D.J. And she wanted to listen to Joey and Uncle Jesse rehearse for their radio show. Plus, she goes to sleep way before midnight and wakes up at six o'clock!"

Allie and Darcy stared at Stephanie in disbelief.

"Didn't you have a late night rap session, like we do at our sleepovers?" Allie asked.

"Are you kidding?" Stephanie asked. "The only late night rapping we did was when Kyra talked in her sleep and I told her to shut up!"

"What a bummer," Darcy said, putting her arm around Stephanie's shoulder.

"Where is Kyra now?" Allie asked, looking around.

"She wanted to go to the library to read," Stephanie said. "So I told her to meet me at my locker after class."

The girls went into the gym and sat on the floor, waiting for class to start. "So you didn't leave the house all weekend?" Darcy asked.

"Well, I had tickets to a Warriors game and I didn't want them to go to waste, so I forced Kyra to go last night. She was bored to tears the whole time."

"Stephanie," Darcy said. "Can I say something? And please don't take this the wrong way."

"Uh-oh. I don't like the sound of that," Stephanie said.

"No, it's nothing bad or anything," Darcy assured her. "I was just thinking. Maybe you should ask Kyra where she wants to go before making any more plans."

"Darcy is right," Allie said. "Maybe Kyra just didn't want to do some of those things you planned, Stephanie. It is her vacation, you know."

Stephanie folded her arms across her chest. "What are you trying to say? That I don't plan fun things?"

"No, that's not what we're saying at all," Darcy insisted. "We're saying maybe you should ask Kyra what she wants to do, then do that. Even if it's different from your idea of having fun."

Stephanie shrugged. "I guess at this point it's worth a try," she said. "But if things keep going like they've been going, I'll be moving in with one of you for the next seven days!"

After school the walk home from the bus stop was uncomfortably quiet.

"So, uh, how was the library this afternoon?" Stephanie asked.

"Pretty good," Kyra answered. "I finished the book I was reading."

"What book?" Stephanie asked.

"*Scarlett*," Kyra answered. "The sequel to *Gone with the Wind*."

Stephanie's eyes widened. "You read that?" she asked in amazement. She had seen that book in the store. It was about as thick as her history text.

"Sure, why?"

"No reason," Stephanie said. "I just thought you liked sci-fi books, like "Star Trek." Did it take you a long time to read *Scarlett?*"

Kyra shrugged. "Kind of. But I read a lot of it on the plane."

"Oh," Stephanie replied. "Was it better than the first one?" It was a dumb question, but she was trying to make conversation.

"No, but it was okay," Kyra replied. "*Gone with the Wind* was one of my all-time favorite books and my very favorite movie."

"I saw that movie on cable," Stephanie said. "I watched it with Uncle Jesse and Aunt Becky a couple of months ago."

"I just love old movies like that," Kyra said.

"They're okay," Stephanie agreed. "But I like new action adventures best. My uncle Jesse and aunt Becky love old movies, too. There's this old film festival going on in Berkeley and—"

"A film festival?" Kyra asked excitedly.

"Yeah, in Berkeley near the university. Anyway—"

"Oh, Steph, can we go?" Kyra pleaded.

Stephanie made a face. "Oh, I don't know—" she replied hesitantly.

"Please, oh, please!" Kyra cried. "I love film festivals—especially of old movies. What's playing tonight?"

"I'm not sure," Stephanie replied. *Citizen Kane*, I think."

"*Citizen Kane!*" Kyra cried. "That's my second favorite movie, ever! Oh, come on, Steph, let's go see it!"

Stephanie thought for a minute. Darcy and Allie had said to try doing some of the activities Kyra suggested. This was probably a better time than any to start. Only Stephanie really didn't care to see *Citizen Kane*. Especially when the newest Keanu Reeves movie was playing right around the corner.

"Sure, no problem," she said finally. "Maybe Uncle Jesse can take us."

"Excellent!" Kyra exclaimed. "I absolutely love this movie. You'll see, Stephanie, you'll love it, too."

Stephanie feigned excitement. "Yeah, I can't wait," she said.

Later on, sitting in the small movie theater in Berkeley, Stephanie wondered why she ever agreed to go. She should have realized that "old movie" meant black and white.

She gazed over to Kyra and saw the intense expression on her face as she watched the movie. Then she turned to Uncle Jesse and Aunt Becky. They seemed just as into it.

Stephanie shrugged, then leaned back in her seat and put her feet over the chair in front of her.

Five minutes later she was fast asleep.

CHAPTER
9

◆ ◤ ◗ ◆

Stephanie quietly unfolded the note Allie had just passed to her. It crinkled loudly in the classroom as Ms. Blattburger scribbled geometric equations on the blackboard.

Stephanie hid the open note in her lap, then casually glanced down to read it.

Steph—I really, really, *really* need to talk to you!!!! Meet me at our usual place. And come alone!!!—Allie

Come alone? Boy, this sounded important. Stephanie wondered how she was going to ditch

Kyra after class and meet Allie at the pay phone by the gym—their usual meeting place.

The bell to end class rang and Kyra was waiting for Stephanie outside the door as planned. Stephanie groaned when she saw Kyra. She couldn't believe Kyra had insisted on wearing heels to school. *Who wears high heels to school?* she thought.

"Hi, Steph," Kyra said. "How was Ms. Blattburger?"

Stephanie made a face. "The usual," she answered. "Boring. I hate geometry."

"I kind of like geometry," Kyra said.

It figures, Stephanie thought to herself. "Anyway, Kyra, do you want to go back to the library next period, or come with me to my health class?"

"I'll come with you," Kyra replied. "I'm totally sick of the library."

Darn, Stephanie thought. They began walking toward the health classroom, when Stephanie suddenly snapped her fingers.

"Oh! I just remembered something! I'm supposed to meet a couple of the girls from the Skate for School committee," she lied.

Kyra made a face at the mention of Skate for School.

"Do you want to come, or should I meet you in class in like ten minutes?" Stephanie asked, crossing her fingers behind her back.

"Um, you go," Kyra said. "I'll meet you in class."

Stephanie practically ran down the hall. "I'll be back in a flash!" she called behind her.

She ran at top speed, way over to the pay phone by the gym on the other side of school to meet Allie. *This'd better be good*, she thought.

Stephanie was surprised to see Darcy waiting there, too. She and Allie both looked so serious.

"What's up?" Stephanie asked breathlessly. "What's with all the secrecy? I'm going to be late for health. And I had to make up this story for Kyra so she—"

"Stephanie! Will you shut up for a second?" Darcy snapped at her.

Stephanie was taken aback. "Well, sor-ry!" she snapped back. "What's her problem?" she asked Allie.

"Listen, Steph," Allie said seriously. "We have something to tell you."

Stephanie waited. "Yeah, well, what is it?"

"It's about Kyra," Darcy said.

Stephanie's eyes narrowed. "What about her?" she asked.

Allie bit her bottom lip. "She did something you're not going to like very much."

"What are you talking about, Allie? What did she do?"

"We had to tell you, Stephanie," Darcy said. "You're our best friend."

"Will you just tell me already!" Stephanie cried.

Allie and Darcy exchanged glances.

"Okay," Allie began. "Here it goes. Last period, Darcy and I were walking through the cafeteria, when we saw Kyra."

"In the cafeteria?" Stephanie asked. "She told me she was going to the art department to make something for Scott."

"She was talking to Brandon," Darcy blurted out.

Stephanie felt her face get hot. "My Brandon?" she asked.

95

Darcy nodded.

"Did you hear what they were saying to each other?"

Allie and Darcy exchanged looks again.

"Tell me!" Stephanie insisted.

Allie took a deep breath. "We heard."

"We *both* heard," Darcy corrected her. "We both heard Kyra ask Brandon to go with her to Skate for School."

Stephanie's stomach tightened. "No way," she whispered in shock.

"It's true, Steph," Allie said, putting a concerned hand on her friend's shoulder.

"Are you positive?" Stephanie asked.

They nodded.

Stephanie threw her book bag to the floor and plopped down next to it. She stared at her friends in disbelief. "How could she do this to me?"

"We're sorry, Steph," Darcy said sympathetically. "I just knew that girl was trouble from the minute I met her!"

"You did?" Allie asked.

"Well, no. I'm just trying to make Stephanie feel better," Darcy admitted.

Stephanie suddenly jumped up and grabbed her book bag. "I'm going to tell her that I know," she said with fierce determination. "I want to see what she has to say for herself!" Whirling around, she marched down the hallway toward her health class, more angry and hurt than she'd ever felt before.

When she got to the classroom, Mr. Kellish was already in the middle of the lecture. Stephanie entered quietly, taking a seat in the last row, two rows behind Kyra. Kyra turned around in her seat and smiled at Stephanie.

Stephanie looked away.

"That class is great," Kyra said to Stephanie as they left the classroom. "Mr. Kellish sure has a lot to say about the dangers of secondhand smoke, don't you think?"

Stephanie didn't respond.

"Back in Atlanta," Kyra went on, "none of my friends smoke. I never even tried it, it looks so disgusting. Don't you think so?"

Stephanie mumbled something under her breath.

"Stephanie?" Kyra asked. "Is something wrong?"

Stephanie spun around and stared Kyra square in the eye. "Yes, something is wrong!" she exclaimed. "And don't tell me you don't know what it is!"

Kyra seemed shocked. "Huh? What are you talking about?"

"You know!" Stephanie snapped.

"Stephanie, did I do something? Are you mad at me?"

"I can't believe you're acting so innocent!" Stephanie bellowed. "I mean, really, Kyra. Did you think I wouldn't find out?"

"Find out what?" Kyra asked.

"About you asking Brandon to Skate for School!" Stephanie gazed angrily at Kyra. "How could you do that to me? You *know* I like Brandon. And you told me you hated skating!"

"I do hate skating," Kyra replied.

"Then why did you ask Brandon to go with you?" Stephanie demanded.

"Steph, you got it all wrong, I swear!" Kyra insisted.

"You mean you didn't ask Brandon to Skate for School?" Stephanie asked.

"No! I mean, yes, but not for me. I did it for *you!*"

Stephanie's mouth fell open. "You *what?*"

Kyra sighed. "I did it for you, Stephanie," she said again. "You see, I was feeling so bad about what I said to you a few days ago about not having a boyfriend. It was really such a horrible thing to say. I didn't mean for it to come out the way it did."

"Go on," Stephanie said.

"Anyway, I remembered how you said you wished you could get up the nerve to ask Brandon out for Friday night, and when I passed him in the cafeteria on my way to arts and crafts, I figured I'd try and make it all up to you by asking him out for you."

"You did?" Stephanie asked in amazement.

"It's the truth! Honest!" Kyra cried.

Stephanie looked at the floor. "So, what did he say?" she asked meekly.

Kyra smiled. "He said he would love to go with us."

"Us?" Stephanie asked.

"Well, I kind of asked him to join our double

date," Kyra explained. "I didn't think you'd mind."

"No! I don't! Wow, he really said yes?"

Kyra nodded.

"What else did he say?" Stephanie demanded. "Tell me every syllable that came out of his mouth!"

Kyra laughed. "Nothing, he just said he'd meet us there."

Stephanie trembled slightly. "I can't believe this," she said in shock. "Thanks! This is the nicest thing anyone's ever done for me!"

"No problem," Kyra replied. "What are friends for? Anyway, I can't believe you would actually think I would ask Brandon out. I have a boyfriend, remember?"

"How could I forget?" Stephanie replied with a hint of sarcasm.

Kyra turned red. "I guess I *do* talk about Scott an awful lot. Sorry."

"It's okay," Stephanie assured her. "I'm sure if I were going out with Brandon, I'd talk about him a lot, too."

"Well, Steph, you *are* going out with Brandon. For one night, anyway," Kyra said with a smile.

Stephanie suddenly went completely pale. "I just thought of something," she said nervously. "What on earth am I going to wear?"

"Don't worry," Kyra assured her. "We'll think of something!"

CHAPTER
10

◆ ◂ ◆ ◆

"Boy, this stuff stinks!" Stephanie exclaimed, un-wrapping the towel from her head. "Is my hair going to smell like this all night?"

Kyra laughed. "No, don't worry. The home perm solution will wash out. Let's see how it came out. Shake your head like this." Kyra bent over and flipped her head back, then primped her curls.

Stephanie did the same thing, but her hair was still wet and tangled.

"Maybe you ought to shower and wash the

gunk out," Kyra suggested. "Then you can let it dry naturally."

Stephanie grabbed her robe and ran to the bathroom. Before jumping in the shower, she examined herself in the mirror. A perm? What was she thinking? She gazed at the mess of tangles on her head. It must have been temporary insanity.

Think positively, she scolded herself as she climbed in the shower. She washed her hair with the special shampoo that came with the home perm kit. Stephanie prayed the perm would look as great as Kyra's and that her new hair would be a hit at the roller rink.

Back in her room Stephanie shook her head till she was dizzy, trying to make her hair dry naturally. Meanwhile Kyra went through the small wardrobe she'd packed for something Stephanie could wear. She held up a straight linen skirt and a cropped top.

"This is cool," Kyra said, showing it to Stephanie.

"Yes, it is," Stephanie said. "But I have to skate tonight, remember? I won't get very far in a skirt like that."

"Oh, right. Hmmm, what about this?" Kyra held up a spandex miniskirt.

"Yeah, sure!" Stephanie said. "Like my father might ever let me out of the house in that!"

"Work with me, Stephanie!" Kyra said. "We have to find something for you to wear tonight."

"What about my black biker shorts and my new tie-dyed T-shirt?" Stephanie asked. She knew she looked good in that outfit and it would be comfortable to skate in, too.

Kyra scrunched up her nose. "Are you kidding? Biker shorts on a date?"

"But it's a Rollerblading date," Stephanie pointed out.

"Still," Kyra replied. "Don't you want to look older? More sophisticated?"

Stephanie thought about that. "Definitely," she replied boldly. "What else do you have?"

"How about my black catsuit?" Kyra asked.

Stephanie shook her head. "Oh, I don't know," she said hesitantly. "It isn't really me."

"You're nuts!" Kyra exclaimed. "It'll look awesome on you."

An hour later Stephanie and Kyra emerged from the bedroom and went downstairs to wait for Allie and Darcy. Joey was in the living room, playing hockey with the twins. They were using rice cakes as hockey pucks.

Joey's jaw dropped when he saw Stephanie. She was wearing Kyra's catsuit and sheer, flowy dress over it. Her hair was a mass of blond curls, and on top of her head was Kyra's black beret.

"Steph, is that you?" he asked, incredulous.

"Yes. Why are you staring at me like that?" she asked nervously.

"No reason," Joey said, trying to sound casual. "You just look so . . . *different.*"

"Your hair is funny!" Alex cried.

Stephanie shot Kyra a look of horror. "Funny? My hair is funny?"

"Calm down, Stephanie," Kyra said gently. "Your hair looks great! He's just a three-year-old."

Stephanie took a deep breath. "I guess you're right," she said. "Are you sure I look okay?" she asked for the millionth time.

"Yes, you look fab! I swear! Wait to see what Allie and Darcy say."

Stephanie was shaking from head to toe. She

felt so strange, so weird, dressed in these clothes with her hair all different and everything. She thought again of the tie-dyed shirt and biker shorts folded in her dresser drawer, wishing she had worn those instead. She was nervous enough about her sort-of date as it was—she didn't need to worry about her outfit, too. She wished D.J. or Becky had been home so she could get another opinion.

The doorbell rang and Stephanie took a deep breath before answering it.

Allie and Darcy gasped when they saw their friend. "Wow, Stephanie! Look at you!"

"Good or bad?" Stephanie asked hopefully. "Be honest!"

They didn't answer at first, and Stephanie began to panic. "Oh, no. You hate it. I'm going upstairs to change."

"Wait a sec, Steph," Darcy told her. "Give us a minute. This is all so new. Okay," she gave Stephanie another once-over. "Good. You definitely look good . . . just different. When did you get a perm?"

"It's temporary," Stephanie explained. "It washes out after a few days."

Allie examined Stephanie's dress. "Can you skate in this outfit?" she asked.

Stephanie nodded. "Do you like it? Should I change?" She was feeling more uncomfortable by the second. "There's still time."

"It's up to you," Allie said. "You look great, but if you aren't comfortable, then—"

"I don't think you should change," Kyra said. "You look terrific. Very sophisticated."

Stephanie took a deep breath. "I hope Brandon thinks so, too."

Stephanie adjusted the cardboard number that hung around her neck.

"Aaachhh, this thing is getting on my nerves!" she complained, untangling its string from a lock of curls.

Allie stared at her friend. "Stephanie, I don't think it's that number card that's bothering you," she said.

Stephanie glanced up defensively at Allie, then sighed. She turned her gaze to the rink, where Brandon and Kyra had been skating together for nearly an hour. "You're right," she said. "This dumb card isn't what's bothering me."

"How long have they been skating together?" Darcy asked.

"Forty-seven minutes," Stephanie grumbled, pushing a curl off her forehead. She stuck her finger inside the beret and scratched her head fiercely. "This stupid hat itches like crazy!" she complained. Finally, she pulled the beret off altogether. As soon as she did, Allie and Darcy backed away.

"What?" Stephanie asked.

Allie and Darcy didn't answer.

Stephanie gasped. "My hair still stinks, doesn't it? Oooh, wait till I get my hands on that girl!" Stephanie growled in Kyra's direction. She slumped back in her chair and folded her arms across her chest.

"What a big flirt," Allie said, watching Kyra and Brandon. "Did you see how she sat down on the rink floor for a full minute until Brandon helped her up? I'll bet she only pretended to fall just so Brandon would help her up."

Now Brandon was actually holding Kyra's hand! Darcy scoffed. "Too bad her boyfriend can't be here to see all this," she said.

"If I had a camera, I'd take a picture and mail

it to him," Stephanie muttered under her breath. She stood and turned to her friends. "I'm going back out there," she said to them. "I'm here to skate for a good cause, and I can't let *her* spoil my night. Anyone joining me?"

"That's the spirit, Tanner!" Allie proclaimed. "I'm right behind you. I can't watch this any longer, anyway."

"Me, neither," Darcy added.

The girls hit the rink and began to skate, trying not to look at Kyra and Brandon every time they skated past. Stephanie was so angry and so frustrated, she began to skate faster and faster. Pretty soon she was skating by herself at top speed around and around the rink.

After a while Stephanie began to get tired. She gazed around the rink, searching for Allie and Darcy.

Instead, Stephanie caught sight of something else. It was Brandon and Kyra. They were leaving the rink.

Finally! Stephanie thought in disgust. *I'd better catch him before he skates with someone else.*

She skated quickly across the rink but braked suddenly halfway there. Brandon and Kyra were sitting at a table for two at the concession stand!

Stephanie felt a lump in her throat the size of a golf ball. Feeling as if she were going to cry right then and there, she lowered her head and skated straight into the ladies' room.

Stephanie stared at her reflection in the mirror. She almost didn't recognize herself. What she saw was a very cute, very curly-haired girl about to cry. The weird thing was, she felt as if she were looking at *Kyra*.

This isn't me, she thought unhappily. *This is me trying to look like Kyra.*

A second later tears began streaming down her cheeks.

Allie and Darcy came rolling into the ladies' room. As soon as they saw Stephanie crying, they rushed to her side.

"Look at me!" Stephanie cried tearfully.

"You don't look bad, Steph," Darcy said. "You just don't look like *you*."

"I know who I look like," Stephanie sniffled. "And she's the last person in the world I want to look like right now. I should have listened to you guys about Kyra. She's nothing but a user and a big phony. She was out to steal Brandon from me all along!"

"That's not true!" a voice said from the doorway.

The girls spun around, and there was Kyra with a look of surprise on her face.

"I'm not out to steal Brandon."

"Ha!" Stephanie replied. She blew her nose and dried her eyes. "Tell me another one."

"Stephanie, I swear. I have a boyfriend back—"

"I know, I know. You have a boyfriend back home. Mr. Perfect. Scott, the world's most romantic guy. Well, maybe since I don't have a boyfriend myself, I don't know very much about romance. But I do know this. It isn't considered romantic to cheat on your boyfriend!"

Kyra turned red. "I am not cheating!" she insisted.

"Oh, you're not?" Stephanie asked. "Then what do you call skating and holding hands with another guy?"

"I don't call it cheating," Kyra said.

"Well, I do!" Stephanie announced. "And I also call it cheating on your best friend when you flirt with the guy you know she likes!"

"You're crazy. I wasn't flirting!" Kyra said.

Stephanie turned to Allie and Darcy. "What do you call it when you glom on to a guy and skate with him for over an hour, laughing and falling all over him?"

"Flirting," Darcy and Allie answered in unison.

Stephanie folded her arms across her chest. "See? And while we're on the subject, how could you ruin my hair like this on such an important night for me? Was it all part of your plan to steal Brandon?"

"I didn't ruin your hair," Kyra protested. "It looks great."

"Maybe, but it stinks! The guys in the skate rental booth can smell it from here!"

"Stephanie, I think you're exaggerating."

"Oh, really?" Stephanie asked angrily. "Well, I'm not exaggerating about this: I don't think we can be friends anymore. Friends don't forget to tell each other things. Friends don't ignore each other. Friends don't skate for an hour with the guy another friend likes. And, most important, friends don't lie to one another. We may look alike—and dress alike," she added, looking down at Kyra's flowy dress and catsuit, "but that doesn't make us best friends." She looked at Allie and Darcy. "And I know what best friends are," she said, "because I have two *real* best friends who would never do any of those things to me."

Stephanie wiped her eyes one last time, then skated past Kyra, out of the ladies' room door and straight to the pay phone to call Joey for a ride home.

CHAPTER
11

◆ ◂ ◼ ◆

"I refuse to eat one more rice cake!" Stephanie announced, pushing the plate of rice cake quiche away from her.

"But that's all there is for lunch today, Steph," her father told her. "Kyra made it herself. From scratch."

"Never mind," Stephanie grumbled. "I'll make something for myself." She pushed her chair away from the table and walked past Kyra without so much as a look.

Stephanie peered into the fridge, looking for something to eat. Something that wasn't made of rice cakes—or rice, for that matter. Finally, she found some leftover canned spaghetti from Nicky's and Alex's lunch the day before.

Stephanie heated the spaghetti in the microwave and joined the others back at the table. It was pouring outside and everyone's Saturday afternoon plans had been ruined. Jesse and Becky had wanted to take the boys on a picnic, Joey had had a basketball game, and Danny had planned to take all the girls sight-seeing. But because of the storm, they were all stuck in the house.

"What time does your flight leave tomorrow night, Kyra?" Danny asked, digging into his quiche.

Kyra gave Michelle some quiche. "Around seven o'clock," she said. "Here, Michelle. There are no animals in this at all. I made it myself."

"Thanks, Kyra!" Michelle said sweetly.

Stephanie rolled her eyes, then adjusted the bandanna she was wearing on her head to hide her hair. Her home perm hadn't washed out in the shower as Kyra had promised.

"Maybe the weather will be nicer tomorrow, Kyra," D.J. said, "and we can do some sight-seeing on your last day here. Wouldn't that be great, Stephanie?"

"Hmmmph," Stephanie grumbled, not looking up from her lunch.

"Did you have a nice visit to San Francisco, Kyra?" Joey asked.

"Oh, yes," Kyra replied. "It was a wonderful trip. You've all been so nice to me."

Stephanie clicked her tongue. *Oh, puh-leeze!* she thought to herself. *What a phony!*

"Excuse me, D.J.," she said to her sister. "Would you pass the grated cheese?"

"Stephanie, the cheese is over by Kyra," D.J. told her.

Stephanie sighed loudly. "Well, then, would you ask Kyra to pass the cheese?"

D.J. stared at her sister strangely. "Why can't you ask her yourself?"

Stephanie's glare was enough for D.J. "Uh, sure, no problem," D.J. replied. "Um, Kyra? Would you pass the grated cheese to Stephanie?"

Without a word Kyra lifted the jar of cheese and slammed it on the table in front of Stephanie. Then she cleared her throat. "D.J.?" she asked. "Will you please ask Stephanie to pass a napkin?"

D.J. stared at Kyra in confusion. "Yeah, I

guess," she replied. "Steph? Can you pass the na—"

Before she could finish, Stephanie grabbed a handful of napkins and threw them across the table at Kyra.

Danny jumped immediately from his seat to pick up the napkins that had fallen to the floor. "Can someone please tell me what's going on?" he asked.

"Nothing, Dad," Stephanie answered grumpily. "Can I be excused from the table?"

"But you barely ate a thing," he pointed out.

"I'm not very hungry," Stephanie replied.

Danny shrugged. "Well, okay, then, I guess."

Stephanie raced from the table and up to her room. She thought about locking the door, but Kyra's things were still in her room and that would be rude. Then she thought about throwing Kyra's things into the hall and locking the door, but she couldn't bring herself to be *that* rude, either.

Stephanie fell onto her bed and stared out the window, watching the rain splatter against the glass. *What a miserable day*, she thought to herself. *What else would follow such a miserable night?*

117

She stared at the dark sky and thought about the disastrous evening before. About how her hair had smelled like rotten eggs and how she'd looked like a total goofball in Kyra's outfit. About Brandon and how he'd barely said a word to her, and most embarrassing, about how she had bawled like a baby in the ladies' room, right in front of Kyra.

Stephanie sighed loudly and rolled onto her side. She pulled a science fiction novel off the shelf and tried to read.

A few minutes later there was a rap on the door.

"It's Kyra. I need to get something out of my bag."

Stephanie scowled. "Come in," she mumbled.

Kyra opened the door and found her bag. She took out the book she was reading and sat on Michelle's bed. Then she stood again and found some things she had borrowed from Stephanie. She carried them over to Stephanie and dumped them on her bed.

"Here," she declared in a snooty voice. "I wouldn't want you to think I *stole* your hair scrunchie and emery board." She spun around and went back to her book.

Stephanie put down her book and went to her closet, pulling out Kyra's catsuit, dress, and beret. She flung them onto Michelle's bed. "You'd better take these," she snapped. "In case you're planning on stealing another boyfriend from somebody tonight."

"For the hundredth time, I didn't steal your boyfriend, Stephanie!" Kyra snapped back. "And Brandon isn't even your boyfriend, anyway!"

"No, but you knew how much I liked him," Stephanie said angrily.

"We were just hanging out," Kyra insisted. "He was asking me about Atlanta."

"Oh, and you just had to hold his hand the entire time, right?"

"Stephanie! I told you I can't skate for my life! I was doing it only for you!"

Stephanie's eyes narrowed. "What are you talking about? You flirted with Brandon for my sake?"

"Oh, never mind!" Kyra said angrily. "You're impossible to talk to. Let's just go back to our books."

"Fine with me!" Stephanie shouted.

"Fine!" Kyra replied.

"Fine!"

"Everything okay in here?" D.J. asked, poking her head in the doorway.

"Fine!" Stephanie yelled.

"Fine!" Kyra yelled, too.

D.J. put her hands on her hips. "What gives?"

Neither Stephanie nor Kyra said a word.

Michelle came into the room with Comet close behind. "What's going on in here? Comet and I are trying to play cards."

Stephanie jumped up from her bed. "I'll tell you what's going on!" she cried. "That girl stole Brandon away from me!"

"I did not!"

"You did, too!"

D.J. stopped them from yelling. "Hold on a second. Stephanie, what's going on here? You two are supposed to be best friends."

"Ha!" Stephanie scoffed loudly. "Some best friend! If Kyra thought I was her best friend, then why didn't she ever tell me about Scott? Or about the play? Or even about hating Chinese food?"

Kyra stared strangely at Stephanie. "I thought I did tell you those things."

"Well, you didn't," Stephanie replied.

"And that's why you're so mad at me? That's what's really bothering you?" Kyra asked.

Stephanie sat back down on her bed. "Well, yeah! It bothers me! That, and other stuff. Like how you don't skate, and how you like geometry, and that you read best-sellers and watch old movies. It's exactly the opposite of me!"

Kyra stood speechless.

Stephanie's eyes filled with tears. "We were supposed to be so much alike, remember?" she asked. "That's what we joked about all the time. But you turned out to be so different from me. You have a boyfriend, you wear lipstick, *everything*."

"We're still alike, Stephanie," Kyra said. "We're just not *exactly* alike. But that's why we got along so well in our letters. We always have fun stories to tell each other. And we both love to write so much. I guess I just forgot to tell you some things, that's all. But not on purpose."

"I don't know," Stephanie said quietly. "I guess I just expected your visit to be different. I wanted us to be the best of friends."

Everyone was quiet.

"I wanted to do all these great things to-gether," Stephanie went on, "but then you didn't like any of them."

"I wanted to do great things, too, but just *different* great things," Kyra said. "I suppose I was upset, too, when you didn't turn out to be ex-actly like me, either."

Stephanie sniffled. "Well, what do we do now?" she asked. They both looked at D.J.

"Why are you both looking at me?" D.J. asked.

"Well, don't you have a solution?" Stephanie asked. "You always have a solution. That's what I pay you for. To solve all my problems."

Kyra laughed. "You're so much funnier than I am, Stephanie. If we were exactly alike, then you wouldn't be so funny."

"Yeah, I guess," Stephanie replied with a laugh. "But what about Brandon?" she asked, remembering why she was so angry in the first place.

Kyra sighed. "I guess maybe I *was* flirting a little with him, but that's only because I miss Scott so much and Brandon reminds me of him. They even look alike."

"Well, I guess there is something we have in common. The same taste in guys," Stephanie said with a chuckle.

"Stephanie, you have to believe me, though. I didn't want to steal Brandon from you at all. Actually we spent most of the time together talking about you!"

Stephanie's eyes widened. "You did?"

Kyra nodded. "Yup. I went on and on about what a great person you are. How you're funny and smart and, of course, pretty and sophisticated! But I think he knew that already."

"Why?" Stephanie asked eagerly. "Why do you think that?"

Kyra smiled. "Because he told me he thought you were cute!"

Stephanie gasped excitedly. "Cute? He said I was *cute?*" She thought she might pass out.

Kyra nodded. "I wanted to tell you last night, but we weren't exactly speaking."

Stephanie grabbed her pillow and gave it a huge hug. "Cute!" she repeated dreamily.

"Hey! I know! I've got a solution!" Michelle suddenly announced.

Everyone looked at her.

"What are you talking about, Michelle?" Stephanie asked.

"I know D.J. usually solves everything, but I know how to make everybody stop arguing."

"Oh, yeah? How?"

"Rice cake sundaes!" Michelle announced eagerly.

Stephanie and Kyra groaned, then looked at each other and burst out laughing.

"I think if I eat another rice cake," Kyra said in between giggles, "I'm going to barf!"

Stephanie laughed. "If I eat another rice cake, you'll be able to use me as a corkboard!"

Michelle frowned. "Well, I thought it was a good idea," she said unhappily.

Stephanie put her arm around her sister. "It is a good idea," she told her. "But what about just regular sundaes? And not tofu sundaes, either," she added with a glance at D.J.

Kyra licked her lips. "Yeah! Some good old-fashioned ice cream sundaes with real ice cream and thick hot fudge, wet walnuts, and—"

"Dad!" Stephanie shouted downstairs, her mouth watering furiously. "Start up the van!"

CHAPTER
12

◆ ◂ ◂ ◆

Stephanie watched sadly as Kyra packed. *It figures,* she thought to herself. *Just when we're starting to get along, it's time for her to go.*

Stephanie opened her desk drawer and pulled out a small wrapped package. Excitedly she handed it to Kyra. "This is for you."

Kyra's eyes lit up. "You bought me a present?" she asked. "Cool!"

"It's a Pearl Jam cassette tape," Stephanie explained. "To listen to on the plane."

"Oh. Uh, thanks," Kyra said, putting it in her bag.

Stephanie's heart sank. "You hate it, don't you," she said.

"No, I don't. Honest," Kyra insisted. "It's just that I don't really like grunge music."

"Sorry," Stephanie mumbled. "I guess I shouldn't have bought it without asking you first. I love Pearl Jam. I guess I just thought . . ." Her voice trailed off.

"Then keep it for yourself, Stephanie," Kyra said. "Since you like them and all."

Stephanie nodded quietly. "Yeah, okay, I guess." She sat on Michelle's bed and watched Kyra fit the last of her things into her suitcase. Then she pulled something out of her canvas bag.

Kyra laughed nervously and handed a soft package to Stephanie. "I don't think you're going to like it," she said.

Stephanie laughed awkwardly when she saw what it was. A beret! "You're right," she said. "It's not really me. So, uh, why don't you keep it and we'll call it even?"

Kyra stared at Stephanie, then laughed. "I guess that's how it is with us, huh?"

Stephanie sighed. "Yeah. Exact opposites!"

She tried to laugh, too, but deep down it made her sort of sad. "I'll wait downstairs for you, okay?"

Kyra nodded.

Stephanie walked slowly down the steps into the kitchen. She wished things had turned out differently between her and Kyra. It was sad, losing a pen pal after all these years. And Kyra really was the perfect pen pal. Well, maybe a *practically* perfect pen pal.

She was absentmindedly staring into the fridge, when suddenly she got an idea.

Excitedly Stephanie grabbed a pen and paper, sat down at the kitchen table, and began writing.

Dear Wilma,

It must be funny to be reading a letter from me when you just saw me a few minutes ago, but I thought this was a good way to say good-bye.

I've been thinking, and I hope that you still want to be my pen pal, even though we don't like the same music or clothes (or books, or hats, or food, or . . . never mind!). We both like to write (Hey, what do you know? Something in common!) and I love getting letters from you.

Anyway, thanks for coming to visit. I can't wait for your next letter.

Love,

Betty (also known as

Cute Stephanie)

P.S. WRITE BACK!!!!!

Stephanie folded the letter and stuffed it into an envelope. She wrote on it, *Please Read on Plane.* Then she ran back upstairs to give Kyra the letter.

Kyra was closing her bag as Stephanie came into the room.

"Stephanie," Kyra said. "I have something else for you."

"I have something for you, too," Stephanie said.

At the very same second, both girls pulled out letters.

Stephanie's eyes widened. "You wrote me a letter?" she asked excitedly.

Kyra nodded. "And you wrote me one?"

Stephanie laughed. "Well, how about that!"

"So much for exact opposites!" Kyra said with a grin. "Go ahead, read mine now."

Stephanie unfolded Kyra's letter.

Dear Betty,

Did I tell you about this great friend I have? Her name is Stephanie Tanner. We don't agree on some things (okay, a lot of things!), but one thing's for sure. She is the best pen pal in the world and I'm going to write to her for the rest of my life. And I hope she keeps writing to me.

Love,

Wilma (Kyra)

P.S. FRIENDS FOREVER

Stephanie smiled and slung Kyra's bag over her shoulder. "Come on, Wilma. You have a plane to catch! After you."

Stephanie followed Kyra downstairs into the dark living room.

Suddenly the lights flicked on, and there was the entire family standing around a huge cake.

"It's a rice cake cake!" Michelle called out excitedly. "Bon voyage, Kyra!"

"Good-bye, Kyra!" everyone sang out.

Kyra got all choked up and a tear trickled down her cheek. "This is so sweet of y'all!" she gushed.

"It was Steph's idea," D.J. said. "Well, not the part about having a rice cake cake."

"I did pick the flavor, though," Stephanie said. "I asked for a strawberry cake."

"Strawberry?" Kyra asked. "Why?"

Stephanie grinned. "Because I hate strawberry cake!"

Kyra laughed. "Thanks, Steph," she said. "This means a lot to me."

Stephanie smiled. "No problem. What are friends for?"

Just then the doorbell rang, surprising everyone. Danny opened the door and in walked a telegram delivery man.

"A telegram? Who's it for?" Jesse asked.

The delivery man read the name on his clipboard. "Miss Stephanie Tanner."

Stephanie raised an eyebrow. "For me?" she asked.

"Yes, from the Georgia Peach Rice Cake company."

Stephanie gasped. "No way!" She ran to the delivery man and ripped the telegram from his hands.

Kyra was confused. "Why is the Georgia Peach Rice Cake company sending you a telegram?" she asked.

Stephanie could barely contain herself. "I must have won!" she cried, jumping up and down.

"Won what?" Kyra asked.

"I've been keeping it a secret from you, Kyra!" Stephanie exclaimed. "But I entered a contest to win a trip to Georgia this summer, and I think I won!"

Stephanie and Kyra threw their arms around each other and squealed with delight.

"Open it already!" Joey exclaimed. "The suspense is killing me!"

Stephanie tore open the telegram. She caught her breath and read out loud. " 'Congratulations, Miss Tanner,' " she read breathlessly. " 'We are pleased to inform you that you are a runner-up in our Win a Trip to Atlanta Sweepstakes.' "

"A runner-up?" Michelle asked.

"What's the prize for runner-up?" Becky asked.

Stephanie read the rest of the telegram, then stared at her family and tried to smile. She fell back on the sofa and put her head in her hands.

"Guess what, guys?" she said meekly. "I just won a hundred cartons of Georgia Peach Rice Cakes!"